OREGON BOUND

TRAIL OF HEARTS BOOK 1

RACHEL WESSON

LONDONGATE PUBLISHING

OREGON BOUND

CHAPTER 1

VIRGIL, ILLINOIS, JANUARY 1852

Oregon, Oregon, Oregon. It was all anyone ever talked about now. Eva wanted to hold her hands over her ears. She hated when her parents fought. They never used to argue so much—not until Pa had been hit by wanderlust. There had been a meeting after church one Sunday. Some people who had traveled to Oregon spoke about how wonderful it was. Several families they knew from Virgil had decided to make the trip.

"Why do Ma and Pa keep shouting, Eva? I hate it. They never used to."

"Don't you worry about them, Becky. You got chores to do. Have you cleaned out the hen house? You know Ma won't be happy if you don't."

"Ma ain't never happy no more."

"Rebecca Thompson, watch your grammar or Pa will be annoyed with you too."

"Ma isn't ever happy," Becky said before sticking her tongue out and walking off.

Eva watched her go. She couldn't chastise her sister for what she was thinking, not when she was echoing her own thoughts. She rubbed her hands down her apron before heading in the direction of the barn. Becky's twin, Johanna was in there, she could hear her singing to the sick calf. Before she got very far, she spotted someone coming to see them and they were in rather a hurry.

She patted back her hair hoping her face wasn't dirty. Maybe it was David Clarke. As soon as the thought popped into her head, she dismissed it. David never called to their home.

The visitor wasn't David but Harold Chapman. Eva tried to hide her distaste for the young man in front of her. He was the son of the mercantile owner and someone her pa felt was a suitable match for her. She shuddered at the thought of those thick lips kissing hers, his fat fingers caressing her body.

"Miss Thompson, you look lovely today. I wish I could spend time with you but I need to speak to your pa."

"Pa's in the house."

"Perhaps you could come with me. What I have to say involves you too."

Eva's stomach churned as she reluctantly followed him into the house. She hoped he wasn't about to propose. What excuse could she come up with?

"Harold, so nice of you to drop by. Eva just took a pie

out of the stove. She is a great cook." Pa smiled at Eva who blushed at his obvious attempt at matchmaking.

She wasn't about to point out her ma had made the pie, she'd just put in to bake. She cut up the pie, in silence, putting a slice on a plate for both men. Her ma came out with cups and the coffee pot. Eva took a seat beside her pa, wishing one or both of her sisters would come in. Her younger brother Stephen was playing in the yard.

"Sit down, Harold. It won't take but ten minutes to have some coffee."

"Thank you, Mr. Thompson. I don't have long. I rode out to tell you Scott Jones has agreed to captain our wagon train. His reputation precedes him as an excellent guide. Have you made your decision?"

Eva saw the mute look of appeal her ma sent her pa but he chose to ignore it. Instead, he shook Harold's hand. "Yes, my boy, we have. The Thompson family will be joining the wagon train and heading west."

Eva looked away as Harold stared at her; the look in his eyes making her very uncomfortable.

"Are your folks traveling, too, Harold?" Pa asked.

"No, they decided to stay in Virgil." Harold didn't sound upset at the forthcoming parting from his family. "Captain Jones has already crossed the plains in both directions at least twice. He is very talented and capable. You need have no fear of anything, Mrs. Thompson, Miss Thompson."

Eva gripped the chair so she wouldn't stand up. She wanted to tell Harold to leave, that they weren't going anywhere. Could Captain Jones ensure her family's safety? Could he mend her ma's heart? Could he stop her parent's arguing? She didn't think so.

Harold drained his coffee quickly before taking his leave. "Please excuse my bad manners but I must ride out to the Freeman's and the Bradley's places to see if they wish to accompany us."

"You are very good to take time out of your schedule to do this." At Pa's compliment, Harold stuck his chest out even more.

"We will be traveling for months. I would prefer we knew the caliber of all the people in our train before we start. We don't want any undesirables traveling with us," Harold said pompously.

Eva knew he measured everyone by the amount of material wealth they had. She had seen first-hand how he treated the poorer children when they had all been in school together. He was a bully. His love of money was one of the reasons she was mystified over why he seemed intent on courting her. Pa wasn't poor but they certainly weren't as well off as Harold's family. There were girls in town who came from wealthier backgrounds. They would be happy to marry Harold.

Eva stole a look at her pa who was staring back at her. She couldn't read the expression in his eyes.

"Quite right, Harold, I am very particular who we keep company with. I have three daughters to protect."

Eva couldn't bear to look at the smug self-satisfied expression on Harold's face. She wanted to excuse herself so she wouldn't have to stand watching him ride off. Pa interrupted her thoughts.

"Harold, wait a minute and I will ride out with you. I want to speak to Tom Freeman about his wagons. I've been reading Horn's Overland Guide. He maintains we need a particular type of wagon."

"Captain Jones has called for a meeting Saturday evening. He wants to discuss all sorts of things. He says we need to be ready to go in three months' time."

"Three months. But we won't have time to get everything ready?"

Eva hated the way her ma's voice trembled. She watched her pa's face seeing the anger cloud his eyes.

"We will be ready and willing to go whenever Jones gives the order. The Thompsons won't be delaying anyone. Come on, Harold."

Pa left without a backward glance.

CHAPTER 2

*E*va waited until Pa could no longer be seen on the horizon before going back into the house. Her ma was sitting at the table, her face in her hands. This was such an unusual sight that Eva had to take a deep breath before she moved closer and gave her mother a hug.

"Don't cry, Ma, everything will be all right."

Her ma wiped her eyes with a corner of her apron. "I'm just being a silly old woman. Your pa is right. Life will be easier in Oregon."

"How does he know? He can't make us leave. I won't go."

Her ma's expression told Eva she had gone too far. Whatever her ma's opinion, she believed Pa's word was the law in the house.

"Eva Thompson, you will do as you are told. Your pa is a good man. He wants only the best for you and your brother and sisters."

"But, Ma."

"Don't back talk me." Her ma walked out the door onto the wraparound porch. Eva followed her but kept silent knowing she needed to let her ma's temper cool a little. She watched as her ma walked around the porch her pa had added to the house shortly after Stephen was born. Her ma had told them often enough what a rough spot the homestead had been situated on when they first arrived. The family had to clear the land of trees, stumps and rocks before they could build a small house. Her pa had extended the house as their family increased. Ma worked hard too. In addition to her small vegetable garden, she also had a flower and herb garden. She liked to sit out on the porch doing her mending while enjoying the different fragrances coming from her garden.

She harvested her crop of vegetables from late May through October. By the end of the growing season the root cellar would be full of anything that could be stored. She dried fruit and canned wild raspberries, gooseberries, blueberries and blackberries. She also pickled vegetables so the family never went without in the long winter months.

The barn was large enough for their needs. Ma churned butter and made cheese from the milk of their cows. Any surplus was sold to the Chapmans. The same with the eggs from the chickens she reared. The family also had a pig and were considered quite comfortably off. The farm wasn't mortgaged unlike a lot of their neighbors. Ma and Pa had worked hard over the years and their mature holdings were proof of their efforts.

Now Pa had decided to sell and start over. All Ma's hard work would benefit someone else. Eva could understand the tears of frustration her ma shed but she found it difficult to understand why her ma didn't fight harder to stay. If she told Eva one more time that it was a woman's duty to obey her husband, Eva thought she would scream. As if reading her mind, her ma spoke again about duty.

"Your pa has made a decision and that's final. Now we have lots to do to get everything ready for the trip. We won't be able to bring all our furniture." Ma's voice quivered as she obviously forced herself to speak. "I shall need your help and that of your sisters to get ready."

Eva had to get to town. She needed to speak to her granny. To beg her to get Pa to change his mind. She also had to see David.

"Ma, can I take the eggs to town? Johanna is in the barn and Becky is cleaning out the hen house. I can check at the store if there is any post."

Ma looked at her but Eva stared at the view across the prairie. She knew her ma probably guessed why she was so anxious to go to town. She held her fingers crossed tightly hoping, just this once, her ma would let her go.

"Go on then but don't be long. Be home before your pa gets back. Wear your bonnet. I am fed up seeing it swinging down your back."

"Yes, Ma, I will. Thanks, Ma." On impulse, she kissed her ma's cheek before taking the basket of eggs and heading in the direction of town. She walked quickly, intent on finding David and telling him what Pa had planned. He would find a way out of this mess.

* * *

SHE COULDN'T BELIEVE the number of people she recognized from Sunday services who were gathered in town. It seemed Oregon fever had affected everyone. She moved through the crowd, to the store. Despite not liking Harold, she loved visiting the mercantile. The Chapmans held a wide range of products. As soon as you opened the door, you were met by the smell of coffee and chocolate mixed with herbs and spices. She walked into the store hoping Mr. Chapman would be out doing his deliveries. Unfortunately, he was standing behind the counter, his ample stomach resting on the ledge. She took a deep breath as she forced a smile. She waited her turn to be served, trying not to cringe when Harold's father took the basket from her hand, his skin touching hers. She didn't like his squinty eyes or his clammy hands. He looked at her like a dog eyed a juicy bone. He added the credit to their bill while remarking it was a pity she'd missed Harold.

"He's dead set on going to Oregon. Wants his ma and me to go with him, but I told him we are staying here in Virgil."

Eva simply nodded. She wanted to escape the store as soon as possible and find David. She'd called to see her granny but she had gone out visiting. She'd have to wait to see her at church on Sunday.

She couldn't find David so, reluctantly, set out for home. She had to get back before her pa did or there would be trouble. As she walked, her feet dragged along the muddy trail.

David was waiting at their tree. He grinned as she walked up to him before pulling her into his arms and kissing her. From the minute she had left home looking for him, she'd longed for him to slide his arms around her waist so she could lay her head on his chest, listening to his heart-beat as he held her close. He bent his head to kiss her allowing her to run her hands through his jet-black curls. He wore his hair slightly longer than was socially accept-able but she loved it.

She enjoyed the sensations at first before remembering they were in full view of anyone who happened to come down the road. She broke apart.

"I been looking for you."

"I called out to your house but Stephen told me you'd gone into town so I was on my way back and decided to wait for you here," David said.

Her heart thumped. He'd never called to the house before. Thankfully, Pa had gone with Harold or there would have been trouble.

"Stop looking worried. I pretended I needed a job. I didn't say anything about you."

She hated the hurt look in his eyes but couldn't help feeling thankful. Pa was in a difficult mood and it was best not to upset him.

"Is that all Stephen told you?" Eva couldn't keep the worry from her voice.

"Yes, why?"

The worried look on his face mirrored her own feelings. She moved closer to him this time not caring if they were seen. "Oh, David, Pa is going to Oregon. Harold came by today and they have both gone to the Freemans to make plans for leaving."

"Harold is going with you. How come?" David's eyes narrowed.

Her heart fluttered. He was jealous, although he had no need to be. She didn't care about Harold. Her face fired up. She hadn't mentioned anything to David about Harold and her pa. Unfortunately, David read into her silence.

"I get it. Your pa feels Harold would make a good husband for you."

"David, don't be like that. What Pa wants and what I want are different. I don't love Harold. I love you." She stood on her tiptoes to put her arms around his neck, pulling his face down for a kiss. She moaned as his mouth captured hers, his evening beard rough on the delicate skin around her lips. She poured everything into her kiss to burn away his worries. He was the only man for her. She wanted to leave him in no doubt about how much she wanted to marry him.

"Prove it. Runaway with me. Tonight," he whispered, his breathing heavier than usual. "We can get married in another town."

Much as she was tempted, Eva couldn't do that to her ma.

David sensed her indecision. He moved away from her.

"Guess your answer is no."

"David, I want to marry you more than anything but... I can't run away. Ma would die of shame." She took a step closer to him reaching for his arm. "Why can't you come to Oregon too?"

"Where am I supposed to get the money for a wagon? You know what they said at that talk. It costs about four hundred dollars for a wagon and supplies, more if you have a family. I have barely twenty dollars and that's only because I bury my earnings so Pa won't find them."

"You don't need a wagon. You can sign on as an extra hand." Eva saw his face harden. "David, don't look like that. I am trying to find a way of us being together."

"Me as a servant. Your pa will love that." David's sharp tone failed to hide his hurt.

"I don't care what my pa thinks."

That wasn't true but she had to persuade David to come with them. She couldn't bear the thought of leaving him behind. "But if you come to Oregon, he will get to know the real you. See you as a hardworking, caring, wonderful man. Once we are in Oregon, we can get married and start our own place. Don't you see? It could be the answer to our prayers."

"And what of Harold?"

Eva's temper rose. "He can go to...you know. I will never marry that man even if he was the last one on earth."

David pushed her hair gently off her face before kissing her tenderly. "Tell me again why I think such a spirited young woman will make me a good wife," he teased.

Eva gave him a halfhearted push. How she wished her pa could see past his prejudices and look at David as a person in his own right. It wasn't his fault his father was the town drunk.

"Does that mean you are going to think about it? You could talk to the train leader. I heard they were looking for more men. They need people to protect the wagons against Indians." Eva shuddered. Stephen insisted on sharing the gory stories in his dime novels. She didn't want to meet an Indian—ever.

"Indians are the least of your worries, Eva. It's disease and accidents that kill most of the people who die on the wagon trains."

She knew that from the books she'd been reading but she didn't let on. Instead, she teased him. "Since when did you become an expert?"

"I started reading up about it after that first talk about going to Oregon. Your pa's face was lit up like a candle. I suspected he might decide to go and I wanted to be ready."

Eva was so proud of David. He had risked everything to go to school and learn to read. His pa used to beat him telling him it was a waste of time, but it didn't stop him learning. He read everything he could lay his hands on since.

"I don't want to hear another word about Oregon. I hate it already." Eva moved closer to him anxious to feel his arms around her. "I don't want to go. I want to stay here and marry you and have a family surrounded by people we know."

"We are having a family," David teased her. However, she could tell by the expression in his eyes he was pleased. He had told her often enough as kids that the thing he wanted most was his own home with a family. His elder brother had run off when his ma had died. There was no one else. He held her close. "Eva, I'll find a way to convince your pa to let us get married. Trust me."

Eva nodded. She trusted David more than anyone else.

* * *

DAVID WATCHED as Eva walked back toward her father's land. He would have accompanied her but if her father caught them together, there would be trouble. Leaning against a tree, David wondered about Oregon. Maybe out there, he could own his own land and raise cattle.

CHAPTER 3

The weeks flew by. There was no sign of Pa changing his mind. In fact, he seemed to be getting more excited by the minute.

"How much land will we have in Oregon, Pa?" Stephen asked before shoveling another mouthful of stew into his mouth.

"Six hundred forty acres in total. It's three hundred twenty acres for Ma and another three hundred twenty acres for me. It will keep us busy, Son."

"Oh wonderful. A bigger farm means twice as many chores for us girls," Becky said glaring at her pa.

Eva waited for his reaction but for once he ignored her sister's outburst.

Stephen quickly continued talking. "It sure will. What are we going to plant? I heard most everything grows in Oregon."

Eva wished she shared Stephen's excitement but she

couldn't. She hated the thoughts of saying goodbye to people whom she'd most likely never see again. Her grandmother was one of them. Pa's mother wouldn't travel with them. Said she'd travelled enough in one lifetime. The next place she was visiting was Heaven. Eva wished she'd change her mind even though she knew the trail would be hard on the old lady. She'd miss her though. Her granny was as strict as Pa in most ways, but she had a much softer side.

She loved going to Granny's house and listening to her tell her stories of growing up in Galway. The way the woman described it, Eva could almost see the green fields and feel the rain on her skin. Her granny had left Ireland with her husband and young family. Eva knew they hadn't left out of choice. Her grandfather had been wrongly accused of a crime and had to go on the run to avoid being arrested and possibly hanged or transported. There had been many violent clashes in Galway between the Irish and their English masters. The authorities wanted to make an example, so they weren't about to listen to pleas of innocence. With the help of friends and family, Paddy Thompson and his family made their way to Cork and from there to America. Her husband and youngest children hadn't survived the trip. She'd arrived in America with only one son and a daughter left out of a family of eight. Despite several offers of marriage, her granny had stayed single. She told Eva it was because the sun stopped smiling the day she buried her husband, Paddy, at sea.

Losing her husband and four children would have

destroyed most women but Granny was determined to provide a secure, safe and prosperous life for her children. Patrick, Eva's father, had worked hard as had her aunt, Anne. Anne had married well, and her husband provided Granny with a small house of her own to live in. Granny said she only tolerated her son-in-law. She hadn't really forgiven her daughter for marrying an Englishman even if he had been born in America to American parents. But given the degree of affection between Granny and Anne's husband, Eva thought Granny was secretly very fond of her son-in-law, but because of her treatment at the hands of a cruel landlord, she wasn't about to admit it.

After the meal was over, she called to see her granny, dragging Becky and Johanna with her. Johanna stayed for a cup of coffee which is more than Becky did. Becky saw Ben and his friends at the store so made her excuses to Granny and headed over to talk to the boys taking advantage of the fact her pa wasn't in town. Johanna had a quick cup of coffee before saying she wanted to check on some children who had been orphaned a month before. They were staying with the reverend and his wife. Johanna had made them a cake. Eva was glad as she wanted to speak to her granny alone.

"Eva, child, I know your heart isn't in this trip but your pa is only doing what he thinks is best for his family."

"Why can't we stay here? I could live with you and look after you. Auntie Anne wouldn't mind an extra pair of hands." Eva knew she was begging but didn't care.

"I'm sure she wouldn't but your place is with your

family. Your pa may act like a hard man but underneath he is still my sensitive little boy."

Eva didn't agree but she wasn't about to argue.

"He needs you, Eva."

"Me? But he says I bring nothing but trouble." She didn't bother to hide her surprise at her granny's words.

Granny's eyes twinkled. "Well, I guess you have more of the Irish fighting spirit than is good in a girl but that will stand to you. Your strength is a gift to your family, Eva. Time will prove that."

"But I will miss you, Granny." Eva sniffed not wanting to embarrass both of them by breaking down in tears.

"I will miss you too. But we can write. The post is better these days. We don't have to wait a year for letters. You can tell me all about your adventures and when you and David get wed, send me a photograph."

"Granny! How did you know about that? Have you told Pa?" Eva knew as soon as she asked the question, Granny hadn't said anything. If her pa thought she was seeing David alone, he would never let her leave the farm.

"Stop fretting. I haven't told anyone. David is a fine young man. Your pa is blinkered."

"He won't listen to me. He wants me to marry Harold."

"Harold Chapman is a self-indulgent clown. I will try talking to your pa again. Might be time to remind him where he came from."

"What do you mean?" Eva asked.

"I ran away to marry my Paddy. My daddy didn't agree with us getting wed either. Paddy wasn't a church-going man. I was as strong-willed as you are and I loved Paddy, so I ran off and we got married."

"You were happy weren't you, Granny?"

"Yes, child, I was very happy. He was taken far too soon but I wouldn't swap those short years we had together for anything." Granny looked wistful. "Paddy was a fine man. Your pa has many of his strengths, but he seems to have inherited some of his grandfather's stubbornness as well."

"Pa has Stephen and Ma has Becky and Johanna."

"Stephen is a child. Johanna is an angel but she isn't cut out for the long trip to Oregon. I wish she could be persuaded to stay here. I would feel better if she did."

"I thought Becky would ask to stay." Eva knew Becky had plans to marry Ben Norwood, the banker's son. She wasn't sure if Ben was aware of the plan or not.

Granny laughed. "Becky couldn't bear being left behind. She views this as a big adventure. You need to keep a close eye on that young lady. She may find her beauty is a curse."

"She just needs to mature a little." Eva felt that she had to stick up for her sister.

Granny patted her hand. "Loyal to the end. That's one of your strongest qualities, Eva. I love your sister but I can see her for what she is. All her life she has used her beauty to wrap everyone around her little finger. She hasn't your depth or Johanna's sensitivity to others. She will end up very unhappy if she doesn't find the right match."

"She believes Ben is the right man for her."

"Ben is a child, even though he is almost twenty. All your sister can see is the packaging. A handsome face won't get her the life she wants."

Eva laughed at the expression on her granny's face. "So who would you match her with then?"

"I haven't met anyone suitable yet. She needs someone special. A strong man with a kind heart but a firm resolve. Someone who can give her the things she needs not the fripperies she wants." Granny stopped talking, closing her eyes as if she had more to say but couldn't.

"Don't mind the ramblings of an old woman. We all have our strengths and weaknesses. Nobody is perfect."

Eva gave her granny an impulsive hug. "You are so wise, Granny. I am going to miss you so much. David suggested we run away but I don't think it's the right time. Although I admit to being tempted."

"Not yet, Eva, darling. Your family needs you on this trip. Once you arrive in Oregon, you will make the right decision. I will pray for you and David and most of all for my son to have his eyes opened."

CHAPTER 4

*D*avid watched Eva from a distance. He wanted to offer to walk her home but he had seen her walk in to town with her sisters. He had to convince her that he would find a way to get to Oregon. He spotted Captain Jones, the man rumored to be leading the next wagon train, coming out of a café.

"Captain Jones, may I speak with you?" David asked politely twirling his hat in his hand.

"What can I do for you?" Captain Jones replied, his tone friendly but his eyes were watchful.

"My name is David Clarke and I want to go to Oregon."

"Doesn't everyone?"

"Yes, sir, I guess they do but I have to go." David tried to hold his voice steady but it was difficult. He was so nervous.

"Why? You in some sort of trouble?"

Too late, David saw why the Captain would think that. He hastened to reassure him.

"No, sir, but my girl is going to Oregon. I aim to marry her and I can't do that if she is there and I am here."

David thought he saw a flicker of amusement in the older man's face.

"I am guessing you don't have the funds to buy your own wagon?"

"No, sir, I have some savings but not enough. I was hoping you would know someone who might hire me on? That is, if you don't have any need for someone yourself. I am a good shot, a hard worker and I know how to keep out of trouble. I am healthy too. Never known a day's sickness in all my life."

"Relax, Clarke, I am sure you are all those things. I don't need anyone though."

David's hopes died in that second. He had to get on the train. He just had too.

"Please, Captain Jones, if there is any way you could help me, I would be grateful."

"Have a word with Mr. Long. He's looking to make the trip. He mentioned he might need an extra pair of hands. No promises mind."

David's hopes swelled once more. He shook Captain Jones' hand firmly.

"Thank you, sir, you won't regret it."

"Okay, Clarke, but do you think I could have my hand back now?"

Belatedly, David realized he was still shaking the man's hand. He laughed self-consciously. "Sorry about that, sir, I am just so excited. I can't tell you what this means to me."

"I think I can guess. But, Clarke, you should prepare yourself. This trip is no Sunday picnic. There are about eight hundred people planning on making this trip. At least one hundred of those will be buried between here and Oregon."

David knew he was staring. He had read the statistics but somehow this man putting them into words struck home more.

"And that's assuming the weather holds, we make good time and don't get caught in the mountains on the wrong side of the snow. So make sure you are ready," Captain Jones finished speaking.

"Yes, sir." David's voice shook slightly. He would follow Eva anywhere but was her pa aware of the risks he was taking?

"Let me know how you get on with Long. See you again."

"Thank you," David said, his mind still considering the statistics the Captain had shared. Maybe going on the trip was a bad idea. He could ask Mr. Thompson to allow Eva to stay here and marry him. As soon as he had the thought, he dismissed it. He knew her pa wouldn't agree and even if he did, what would he and Eva live on. He didn't have enough savings to buy a place in Virgil. He couldn't move Eva into the shack he shared with his father. In Oregon, he could claim land and build up a farm. It would take hard work but it would be worth it. He closed his eyes, picturing him and Eva sharing a home with their children. It was a nice dream. He had to find this Mr. Long and turn it into a reality.

CHAPTER 5

*E*va collected her sisters and they made the trip home together. Becky chatted incessantly the whole way home not seeming to notice Eva didn't say anything. Johanna didn't add much to the conversation either but then she never did.

Eva had some chores to do in the barn so the twins went ahead of her. When she reached the house, she could hear the twins arguing above in the loft. She glanced at her ma but she was reading her bible. It was almost as if she couldn't hear her daughters but that couldn't be true. It was more likely she was trying to find answers to her heartache.

Eva climbed the stairs to the loft.

"Becky stop, you are scaring me. Eva, make her stop, please."

Eva got into bed beside her younger sisters. "Becky,

can't you see whatever story you are telling Johanna, she's scared."

"I was just trying to prepare her for the trek to Oregon," Becky said resentfully.

Eva knew by her tone she had been trying to scare Johanna. It wasn't hard to do and often Eva got irritated by how easily upset Johanna was. But tonight was different. Since Pa had decided they were traveling to Oregon, feelings were running high. Ma was particularly short with her children, and Johanna had caught the brunt of it over the last few days.

"She told me about some people who got lost and ended up being caught by the snow. They didn't have anything to eat so when their children died, they..." Johanna started sobbing uncontrollably. Eva gathered her in a hug. "Hush, Johanna, you will have Ma and Pa up here if you keep that up. Becky was only trying to scare you. That story isn't true."

"It is so. Harold Chapman was telling some boys about it at the store earlier. He knew everything about it," Becky insisted.

"Harold Chapman doesn't know everything. Now shush up and go to sleep or I will tell Pa you have been making eyes at Ben Norwood."

"Have not. You're real mean, Eva Thompson. I hate you."

"She is not mean, Becky. You are. You told me those horrible stories and now when I think of those poor..." Johanna wasn't able to continue as the crying took over.

"That's quite enough you two. Go to sleep. We all have an early start in the morning. Ma needs our help getting ready."

As their elder sister, the twins knew they should do as Eva said.

Eva pulled the patchwork cover up higher so it covered her shoulders. She didn't want to think about the Donner party and could strangle Harold for telling people about it. Why give people gruesome details when they could be facing similar perils in a matter of days? He was such a child.

"Eva," Becky whispered.

"Becky, go to sleep, I have had enough for one night."

"Please don't tell Pa about Ben. You know what he is like. He will cane me for sure."

"I won't tell so long as you remember Johanna isn't as worldly wise as you."

Nobody would guess her sisters were twins. Johanna was quiet and peaceful. Becky was the complete opposite. It was never boring with her around. Both got into trouble regularly with their parents. Johanna for daydreaming and forgetting what she should be doing. Becky for flirting with boys and behaving like a tomboy. They were sixteen now, so both of them should be more mature. Johanna still had a childlike innocence about her. She was super sensitive and easily upset. Animals trusted Johanna and she seemed to understand them. Ma said she was too caring for this world. Eva knew her ma worried about Johanna almost more than she did about Becky which was saying something.

She was only two years older than the twins but sometimes she felt more like their mother. How would they fare on the trail? Would all of her precious family reach Oregon safely? She had read books similar to the ones Harold had, although she would never admit that to him. She knew the history of the Donner party, but it wasn't that which frightened her. It was the fact that one in ten people traveling to Oregon died along the route. Not due to being trapped by snow but by things you couldn't see, like cholera, dysentery and other illnesses. She buried her head under the covers in a bid to block out her thoughts. It was a long time before she drifted off to sleep.

CHAPTER 6

The fire behind Eva was making her uncomfortably hot, but Ma wanted to dry off some wet clothes. Ma had sorted through the items she wanted to bring with her to Oregon. The rest had been washed, ready to be donated to the church for the poor.

Pa was sitting down smoking his pipe while reading his guidebook. The women were all stitching—something Eva hated passionately. She bit her lip to prevent crying out as the needle pricked her skin once more. Ma had already told her off for her stitching on the double canvas sacks they were making. They needed them to store the large quantities of food recommended in the guidebooks. Becky and Johanna were sewing in silence, they were both better than her at any type of needlework.

Someone knocked at the door. Her pa opened it to admit Harold delivering the large order Pa had placed at the store. As Eva helped to move it from Harold's wagon into the house, she bet Mr. Chapman was rubbing his hands with glee at the size of the orders each of the wagon parties were placing at the store. One hundred lbs. of flour, 70 lbs. of bacon and 30 lbs. of hardtack were recommended for each adult. On top of that, Pa had ordered beans, rice, coffee, sugar, baking soda and vinegar. Ma already had plenty of dried fruits ready.

No wonder Harold had plans to build a huge store in Oregon. Between the profits his pa was sharing with him now and the money he planned to make by selling additional stores along the route, he would be a very wealthy man.

Harold told Pa about the stores he would be bringing on the train. It was the first time Eva saw Pa lose his temper with the younger man. Not the last she hoped.

"You heard what Captain Jones said. You can't bring more than what he recommended. You will be forced to discard it."

"I won't. You heard the stories. So many people don't read the guidebooks and end up having to buy provisions at the forts. This way I can keep them supplied on route and they will be so grateful they won't mind paying extra." Harold's face was a picture of smug satisfaction. Eva had to look away as it made her feel ill.

"You are going to take advantage of the good families traveling with us?"

At the look of disgust on Pa's face, Harold faltered.

"It's business. Supply and demand. They'd pay higher prices at the fort," Harold changed tactic. "I have good reason to try to make as much money as possible. I hope to have a wife and family in Oregon, and I want her to have the best in everything."

Eva pretended not to notice how his gaze had landed on her. Everyone knew who he meant as his wife. She risked looking at Pa. His temper seemed to have dissipated somewhat, though he still looked annoyed.

"Just make sure your prices aren't too high. I don't want anyone complaining of being taken advantage. Not if they intend on becoming part of my family."

Harold's cheeks reddened but he wisely stayed silent. Eva pretended she hadn't heard anything. Neither man would appreciate her input, and she was learning to pick her battles with her pa.

Eva had to leave. She couldn't stand being in such a small space with Harold any longer. Their home wasn't large at the best of times but with Harold and all the stores for the trip, it was almost too small to breath.

"Pa, can I go see Granny now, please? I said I would."

"Have you done all your chores?"

"Yes, Pa." Eva forced the biggest smile onto her face. "Please, Pa. I can walk. The fresh air and exercise will do me good."

"I can drive you, Miss Thompson."

Eva's stomach dived. She didn't want him driving her anywhere.

"Alone?" Ma asked. "My daughter doesn't travel with any young man alone. She has a reputation to protect."

Eva bit her lip waiting for her pa's response.

"Go on then. Tell Ma I will come see her on Sunday after church."

"I will, Pa. Thank you."

Eva hurried off before her pa could change his mind. She didn't like the speculative look in Harold's eyes. He may have guessed it wasn't only her granny she planned on seeing.

* * *

As luck would have it, David was working at Granny's house.

"Hello, what are you doing here?" Eva said happily.

"Your granny had some chores she wanted doing. You look real pretty today."

Eva smiled. She guessed her granny had David working at her house on purpose. She wished her pa was more like her granny.

"Eva, there you are. I was thinking you had forgotten about me. I made some sugar cookies. Come inside, David, and sit with us."

Eva could have kissed her granny. Instead, she busied herself making some coffee. David washed up before coming into the kitchen and taking a seat.

"So, have you managed to find yourself a spot on the wagon train yet, David?"

"Yes, Granny Thompson."

Eva's eyebrows shot up. She hadn't heard.

"A farmer by the name of Long needs help. He has a

wife and daughters but no son. He wants me to hunt and look after his animals. In return I can travel with his family."

Initially, Eva was delighted, until he mentioned daughters. David would be traveling in close proximity to the Long family.

"Daughters? What age?"

"No idea. I didn't ask." David dunked his cookie into his coffee.

Granny laughed at the look on Eva's face. "Eva, darling, I think we both know David only has eyes for one young woman."

David's face went as red as Eva's felt.

"You two would think you were the first couple to ever fall in love. I remember when I first met my Paddy. Such a fine handsome man he was. He had the smile of an angel and the charm of the devil." Granny's eyes looked misty. Eva didn't want to breathe for fear of breaking the spell. David winked at her before turning his attention back to her granny. The old woman took a deep sigh. "It's a difficult thing when families don't agree with the choices you make. Have patience. Don't do anything silly to make their fears come true. Give them time to come around to the idea of you as a couple."

"And if they don't?"

"Sweetheart"—Granny took her hand—"if your pa hasn't come to his senses by the time you get to Oregon, then by all means follow my example and elope." She squeezed her hand, her eyes sending a message of love stronger than anything she could say. Eva choked back the lump in her throat. She was going to miss her terribly.

David spewed his coffee everywhere at the mention of eloping. He coughed and spluttered. Eva and Granny exchanged a grin before Eva hit David hard on the back to help him recover. She may have hit him a little harder than necessary but that was to get back at him for mentioning the Long girls.

CHAPTER 7

*D*avid called back to see Granny Thompson a couple of days after Eva's visit. She owed him some money but that wasn't his reason for calling. He figured she'd be lonely at the thought of her son and his family going to Oregon.

He had chopped extra firewood for her, stocking up her woodhouse out back. Granny's daughter and her son-in-law looked after her but sometimes they were out of town. He didn't want to risk anything happening to Eva's granny. She was one of the few people in town to be kind to him right from the very first time he had met her. He'd been about eight, starving and grieving for his ma and baby sister. Not only had the old woman given him food, a bath and a place to sleep for a couple of nights, but she had given his old man an earful about looking after him. It worked for a while. His pa had got a job and things were looking up. But Pa ended up back in the saloon and that was the end of the job.

Over the years, Granny Thompson looked out for David as much as she could. She fed him, knitted him jumpers and helped him with his school work. It was because of her he could read and write. He used to pretend she was his real granny. He called her Granny just like Eva did. He would really miss her when he left for Oregon.

"That you, David?"

"Yes, Granny. I got your wood all done and fixed up that chair."

"You didn't have to do that, lad."

"I know, but it was driving me mad, the way it rocked when I sat down." David's cheeks flushed. Granny could spot a liar ten towns away or so she told everyone.

"I am glad you came to visit. I wanted a quiet chat with you."

David's heart hit his stomach.

"Don't look so fearful. It ain't bad news. I want to give you something. Two things, actually."

"Granny, you already gave me everything I need."

"Shush up. Don't interrupt your elders." Granny looked at him, her stern tone not quite matching the twinkle in her eyes. "I've known you a long time, David Clarke, and I believe you are the right match for my granddaughter. In time my son will come to see it. At least I hope he will. So I want you to promise me you will do everything you can to keep safe during your trip. You eat healthy mind and be careful what you drink. If that dog of yours won't drink something, you don't force him. Dogs got more sense than humans at times."

"Yes, Granny."

"I got you a present. I don't want any ifs or buts. I want you to go to the store and collect a new pair of boots. Make sure that snake behind the counter gives you the best they have. I paid for them already but I don't put it past him to fleece you."

David was overcome. He'd never owned a pair of new boots before.

"Thank you, Granny."

"Got to keep your feet clean and dry. My daddy told me that and he was never wrong. Well, apart from his views on my Paddy which brings me to my next gift."

David watched as the woman wriggled with her finger. She got up and rubbed some butter into her hand. With a sigh, her ring came off. She gave it a quick rub in her skirt, a quicker kiss and handed it to him.

He stared at it and then looked up to see her eyes glistening.

"I can't take this," David protested.

"You can and you will. I want you to give it to Eva. It's never been off my finger, not from the first time Paddy put it on there. There have been times I was tempted but Paddy said to keep it until the day came it could do more good elsewhere. I've no need of it. I have my love for Paddy in here." She struck her chest. "You give it to my grand-daughter. Make her as happy as my Paddy made me.

41

Promise?" Granny folded the ring into David's hand, holding her own hands over his.

David nodded, her kindness leaving him speechless.

"You are a decent man and never forget it. I couldn't be prouder of you, David Clarke, if you were my own flesh and blood. I am glad my Eva had the sense to fall in love with you. Be happy. Now go on with you. I'm fit for my bed."

David knew she wasn't really going to her bed but wanted him to leave as she hated people seeing her get emotional.

He hugged her close. "I love you like you were my own family. Thank you."

He left as his own tears were threatening to spill over and that would embarrass both of them.

CHAPTER 8

"Ma, can you not talk Pa into letting me stay with Granny for a few weeks before we leave. Mrs. Chapman said I could help her in the mercantile. It would be good experience and I will get to earn some of my own money."

"I think your granny would enjoy having you close by. Let me talk to your pa."

"Thanks, Ma." Eva gave her ma a hug before returning to her needlework.

* * *

Eva couldn't believe her pa had agreed to her staying with Granny in town and working in the mercantile for a couple of weeks before they departed.

"It will give you a chance to earn some money. You will also get to know Mr. and Mrs. Chapman better," he said.

She didn't argue. Eva was happy earning money. She and David would need it when they settled in Oregon. She knew her pa hoped her and Harold would grow closer.

Eva made sure she was never alone with Mr. Chapman. As she told her ma, he made her feel very uncomfortable. She didn't eat with the Chapmans preferring to return to her granny's house. But sometimes, when the store was particularly busy, Mrs. Chapman made them a quick sandwich for lunch rather than closing. It was at these times Mr. Chapman often made excuses to sit beside her. He always moved too close. If he didn't sit beside her, he commented on her appearance. Once, she had heard him saying how well she was made for having children. Mrs. Chapman had apologized to Eva later saying her husband had got carried away as he couldn't wait for grandchildren. Eva felt sorry for Mrs. Chapman, not only was she married to an oaf but he ridiculed her at every opportunity.

* * *

ONE DAY, a harassed looking young woman came into the store carrying a young baby. Eva recognized her from church services, although she didn't know the woman's name. She brought in some butter and a few eggs. She waited at the back of the queue for Mrs. Chapman to serve her. Eva only noticed as she let a number of men who came in later be served before her. Unfortunately, Mrs. Chapman must not have seen her, as she said she had to pop upstairs for something. That left Eva, Mr. Chapman and the woman alone in the store.

Eva watched Mr. Chapman as he served the lady. He held up the eggs to the window as if needing more light. He tasted the butter with his finger. Then he gave her a figure, from her reaction one much lower than she was expecting. She looked at Eva, her eyes full of despair and hopelessness.

"Please Mr. Chapman, I have three young'uns and the baby. They are growing boys and are always hungry. Since Joe..."

"Ran off with the saloon girl, didn't he? Wonder why? I would imagine being married to a fine figure of a woman like you would keep any man happy."

Eva watched from where she was supposed to be cleaning, as the woman wrapped her shawl tighter around her shoulders as if it was a shield.

"I need these items." She pointed to the small number of items on the counter. "Can I put the rest on credit? I will pay you at the end of the month when I sell off some animals."

"No credit. Your husband left an outstanding balance. It has to be cleared in full," Mr. Chapman said sharply.

"But my children are hungry. I can't, I mean I don't..."

Horrified Eva realized the woman had started to cry. She went to move but Mr. Chapman had already come out from behind the counter. He moved closer to the woman, putting his arm around her shoulders handing her a handkerchief. "Please don't ruin your pretty face by crying, my dear. I am sure we can come to an arrangement."

Eva willed Mrs. Chapman to return. She had an idea of what Mr. Chapman was suggesting. Judging by the look on the woman's face she was horrified. But she was also desperate. She looked at the babe she was carrying before turning her attention back to Mr. Chapman.

"An arrangement? I could take these things?"

"Certainly. I will drop them out to your place later this evening. I assume that would be agreeable."

The woman looked at Eva briefly, the blush on her neck rising to cover her face. She ducked her head and murmured something Eva couldn't hear. She had heard Mr. Chapman, though, and it turned her stomach at how sickly nice he sounded. "Why don't we add a couple of extra things to your list. Some candy for the children for instance."

"No. I don't have money for that."

"That's no problem," Mr. Chapman replied.

"Of course it isn't, Maria, dear. How have you been coping? I keep meaning to call out to see you and the little ones but we have been so busy." Mrs. Chapman's voice made everyone jump. Nobody had seen her come down the stairs. Mr. Chapman moved away from the lady very quickly.

Maria looked so embarrassed and uncomfortable, Eva had to say something.

"I could come with you to drive Mrs. Brownlow home, Mrs. Chapman. Mr. Chapman kindly agreed to hold her credit open until she sold some animals. She has quite a few things to carry and with the baby and all, it would be nice to give her a lift."

"That won't be necessary. I always do the deliveries," Mr. Chapman said.

Eva's knuckles turned white as she clasped her hands by her skirt in an effort not to tell Mrs. Chapman what had transpired.

"That's a wonderful idea, Eva. I have missed seeing Maria's boys. They are such cute young things. We will go right now. We deserve some time off," Mrs. Chapman said firmly. "Can you put the candy you promised Maria into the bag as well please, Harrison?"

Eva hid a smile as Mrs. Chapman ignored Mr. Chapman's expression of outrage.

"I got some nice tinned items in last week. A treat for you and the children. You will also need some more flour, some yeast, sugar and a variety of spices." Mrs. Chapman continued adding things to the bundle which grew by the second.

From the looks of things, Mrs. Chapman had heard everything, and was intent on making her husband pay a very heavy price.

"Eva, I don't know if you ever tasted Mrs. Brownlow's cooking but she makes wonderful cookies. They melt in your mouth."

Mrs. Brownlow looked up at that moment. Eva saw the hope glistening in her eyes. She watched Mrs. Chapman walk out of the store before she moved closed to Mr. Chapman.

"You better pray my Joe doesn't come back. If he hears what you tried to do to me, he'd beat you black and blue. I got brothers who would shoot first and ask questions later just in case you get any more disgusting ideas."

Eva grinned at the look on Mr. Chapman's face. That told him.

* * *

SHE ENJOYED the trip with Mrs. Chapman and Mrs. Brownlow. She played with the baby while the two women talked about this and that. She saw for herself how skinny Mrs. Brownlow was when they arrived at her homestead and she took the shawl off. She must have been giving her food to the boys, as they didn't appear to be starving. Mrs. Chapman was clucking around her like a mother hen.

"If your mother could see you now, Maria, she would have a fit."

"Ma never liked Joe but I didn't listen, did I? Now look at me. Twenty-five, no man and four young'uns to look after."

"He might come to his senses yet."

"If he ever darkens my door again, it will be the last thing he does. My brothers will make certain of that. I don't miss him. He was a lazy sod but the boys miss him so badly."

"What are you planning on doing?" Mrs. Chapman asked.

"Captain Jones, he's the man taking one of the wagon trains to Oregon. He came out to see me—I think the preacher asked him to. Anyway, he said there were going to be a lot of people looking to buy land here in Virgil. Some already tried the trail but didn't like it and turned back. He's going to help me sell them the livestock and this homestead."

'But Joe isn't here to sign the papers."

"He already signed them. The day he left with that..." Maria Brownlow didn't need to use the word, they both knew what she meant.

"What will you do?" Mrs. Chapman asked.

"I'm going home. I never liked it here. I mean you and some of the other ladies were friendly to me and I will never forget your kindness. But I want to go back to Clover Springs. That's where I was happiest. Bill, my older brother, he is going to come with me. I can start over."

Mrs. Chapman gave Maria a big hug. "I wish you all the best, my dear. You are a wonderful mother as these fine children show. And I want you to forget all about your bill at the store. I am sure my husband has wiped it clear already."

Eva knew then Mrs. Chapman had heard the entire conversation.

CHAPTER 9

*W*hen Eva got home after her stay in town, there was a surprise waiting for her. A large wagon was parked outside their home. Her ma looked happier than she had earlier. Her pa was complaining it had cost more than the $110 dollars he had budgeted.

"People are getting greedy. They know the best wagons for the trail are prairie schooners and they are taking advantage by increasing their prices."

Eva wanted to tell him to sell it on to someone else and let them stay living here but she wasn't that brave. Instead, she stayed quiet and listened as Pa reassured Ma the canvas cover was watertight and would protect her belongings. The wagon wasn't the only thing Pa had bought. He sold some of their horses and used the money to buy oxen. Her younger brother was trying to get the oxen to move quickly but he didn't have the strength to make them go

51

anywhere. Becky and Johanna were holding their sides laughing as their brother tried to get a particularly large animal to move.

"Eva, your ma will need your help over the next week. Johanna and Becky will help too. We got to pack everything up so it can be loaded properly into the wagon. Every bit of space must be used."

"Yes, Pa," Eva said but she didn't look up from the ground. She was surprised when he moved toward her.

"Daughter, let's take a walk. It's been a long time since we did that together."

"Can I come too?" Stephen said having gotten tired of the Oxen already.

"Not this time. I want to speak to Eva Louise alone."

Eva Louise. She was in trouble. He only ever used her full name when she'd done something wrong. She struggled to keep her breathing calm as she walked alongside him. His silence made her feel worse. She wondered if she should speak first but what would she say?

"I spoke with your granny. She told me…"

Eva's heart missed a beat. What had Granny done now?

"She said you were very upset about leaving town. I appreciate you may think leaving is the worst decision I've made but as head of this household, the decision is mine. I don't expect you to like it but you will accept it. Your ma needs your help and support. The other children look up to you."

Eva walked along in silence. She kept walking not realizing her pa had stopped.

"Eva."

She turned.

"Yes, Pa?"

"Are you listening to what I said."

"Yes, Pa."

"So are you going to put the black mood behind you? This is an adventure. It will be exciting and something you can tell your children and grandchildren about."

"I'll miss Granny." Eva couldn't keep the tears from making her voice shake.

Unexpectedly, her pa put his arm around her shoulders, the closest thing to a hug he had done in a long time.

"I will too. But your granny, of all people, knows we have to make our own way in this world."

I will, Pa. By marrying David. But Eva didn't say anything out loud. There was no point.

"We best get back. Your ma will have dinner ready."

They walked back to the homestead in silence. Dinner was waiting and her siblings were so excited about the wagon and the trip their chatter filled the awkward silence between Eva and her parents.

* * *

EVA PRETENDED NOT to notice her ma's occasional sniff as she wrapped up a piece of china. Eggs, china and other fragile items were packed in barrels of cornmeal.

"Where are the twins? I thought they were supposed to help," she asked on the first morning.

"I sent them into town. Johanna is as likely to break the eggs as pack them and Becky...well, she isn't the best at organizing things how I like them."

Eva thought her ma's excuse was a bit feeble. She wondered if it meant Ma wanted to speak to her in private too. Heart beating quickly, she folded the family's good clothes and lined a large trunk with them. They wouldn't be needed until they arrived in Oregon.

"Put the bolts of cloth in there as well, please, Eva. I don't want any of those Oregon folk thinking we can't afford new clothes."

As soon as the trunk was half full, her pa moved it onto the wagon. She could understand his logic, it would become very heavy once full. But it meant she had to climb in and out of the wagon to finish packing.

"Ma, do we have to wear skirts when traveling? Some of the women traveling are going to wear bloomers."

Her ma's face looked like she had just asked to travel naked.

"Eva Thompson, what on earth has got into you? Of course, we will wear skirts, although we will have to take them up an inch or two so it's easier to walk. But I won't have my girls wearing boy's pants. Not now, not ever."

Eva was sorry she'd asked. Her ma was real annoyed now.

"What's more, you will wear a sun bonnet every day. I

am not having you arrive in Oregon browner than an Indian. Do you hear me, girl?"

Eva nodded but was saved from replying by Stephen.

"Ma, will we see Indians, real life ones?"

"Stop annoying your ma, Son. Can't you see she's busy."

Stephen didn't see the look that passed between his parents but Eva did. She had heard them discussing the possibility of attacks again last night. She'd wanted to tell them what David had said, but they wouldn't have listened.

She continued rolling the feather beds and other necessities in canvas cloth. She packed them neatly into the wagon. Ma put the box carrying plates, bowls and cutlery into the back. Standing upright she put her hands on her hips surveying the contents of the wagon.

"That's it, I think. There's barely room for your pa's tools."

"He tied them on the sides already, Ma. He has his scythe and hoe on that side with the tin pitcher of grease for the axles. He's going to hang a barrel and some rope on the other. I think every inch of space has been used."

Ma nodded as she looked around her. The family's everyday clothes would hang on hooks fixed to the hickory bows of the wagon. She had put their toiletries in a couple of pockets she had sewn into the canvas covering. Above her hung a lantern and a shotgun. Eva noticed her ma's look of distaste. Her ma hated guns but she had no choice. Pa had insisted everyone learn to use the rifle including Stephen. He'd thought it was brilliant. Eva and Johanna didn't believe they would ever be able to use it let alone kill anyone. Becky had become an excellent shot much to her parents' consternation. Eva couldn't help feeling sorry for her sister. No matter how hard she tried, she was never good enough at the things her parents thought she should be.

CHAPTER 10

a few days later, the family headed back into town for another meeting about Oregon. Eva couldn't understand why they all had to go. Pa could tell them everything they needed to know.

"Hurry up, Eva, we will be late. I want to get a seat in the front row."

"I know you think this is a big adventure but some of us don't want to go, Becky," Eva snapped back.

"You are being a real stick in the mud. This is a chance for us to live. To see new things. To get away from dull and boring Virgil. I can't wait. Can you help me with this, please?" Becky smiled her widest smile and winked making Eva laugh. You could never stay in a bad mood for long when Becky was in good humor. Eva helped put her sister's hair up.

"Why are you wearing your best gingham? It's a

meeting not a party," Eva said noticing her sister's dress for the first time.

"Yes, but Captain Jones is going to be there and our Becky wants to make the right impression, don't you, Becky?" Johanna teased.

Eva was surprised to see Becky turning bright red. She thought her sister liked Ben, but it seemed Johanna had more current knowledge.

"Since when? I thought you liked Ben," Eva said.

"Ben's a boy. Captain Jones is a real man." Becky sighed dramatically.

"You won't need a boy or a man if Pa catches you making eyes at anyone. You know that better than most." Johanna gave her hair a quick check before climbing down the ladder to the room below.

"She's such a goody two shoes. Makes me sick," Becky said nastily.

"Come on, Becky, put a smile on your face. You don't want to scare Captain Jones off with a face like that."

Eva poked her sister in the ribs before making her way downstairs and out into the wagon. They wouldn't be late for the meeting. Her pa was nearly as eager to get there, as Becky but for different reasons.

* * *

Eva sat in the meeting listening to Captain Jones explain his reasoning for the week's delay in departure. The heavy rains they had all appreciated were the reason. Although the grass was abundant for the animals, the ground was muddy thus hampering the speed of travel. The rivers were also swollen making them more difficult to cross.

"I say we go anyway. The sooner we get going the better," Harold shouted, and a few in the crowd showed their agreement.

Eva watched Captain Jones' face. He didn't appreciate being questioned so publicly.

"We go when I say so and not before," Captain Jones said sternly. "Anyone who has a problem with my rules, go find another wagon train. I won't have my orders questioned."

The crowd murmured but nobody challenged the captain.

"You all have your instructions regarding the packing of your wagons. Do not over pack. The trail to Oregon is littered with people's belongings for a reason."

Someone in the crowd muttered but stopped at a glare from Captain Jones.

"There are seventy wagons in this train. I owe it to the group as a whole to get you to Oregon before winter. We don't want a repeat of the Donner experience." Captain Jones surveyed the group in front of him. "I expect you all to keep up. I will not wait for anyone. Is that clear?"

Nobody said anything. Eva could see shock on a number of faces.

"What if someone gets ill?" A man asked.

"They continue traveling or they fall behind. We have a very tight timeframe. We can't afford to waste time."

"We can't leave sick people behind to fend for themselves. That isn't right." Too late, Eva shut her mouth. She couldn't believe she had spoken out loud. Johanna squeezed her hand. A glance at her face told her Johanna agreed with what she had said. Her pa's thunderous expression told her he would punish her later.

"Miss..." Captain Jones seemed to be waiting for her name.

"Thompson... Sir," Eva muttered.

"Miss Thompson, while I expect sensitivity from our female travelers, I also require full obedience to my rules. To make you feel better, I should clarify. Where possible, we will not leave the sick behind."

Eva sighed with relief.

"Sometimes it is a necessity for the safety of the larger group. Do you understand?"

"I understand but I don't necessarily agree," she said haughtily.

She thought she saw a hint of a smile in his eyes but it was gone in a flash.

"That's alright, Miss Thompson. I don't expect agreement. But you will follow my orders or you can stay behind right here in Virgil."

"She'll follow orders, Captain Jones. You won't hear another word from her," Pa answered after taking Eva's arm in a vice-like grip.

The meeting broke up soon after. Eva thought she might be able to slip away to speak to David for a few minutes but her pa was not in a good mood. She was in trouble for speaking out like she did so she didn't risk it. Becky wasn't smiling either. Her earlier good mood had vanished when Captain Jones referred to her as one of the children. Stephen was upset because their departure had been delayed. Johanna was the only one who seemed totally unaffected by the meeting. Eva wished she could be more like her sister. She lived in her own world most of the time, but she seemed happier than the rest of them.

It rained heavily as they traveled home. Getting wet didn't make anyone feel better. When they got home, Pa sent Eva to bed without supper for embarrassing him at the meeting.

The rain continued for the next week keeping everyone stuck indoors for hours at a time. Tempers were short. Arguments were quick to break out leading to a horrible atmosphere. Eva blamed everything on Oregon and couldn't wait to escape the house.

CHAPTER 11

VIRGIL, APRIL 14, 1852

*D*avid checked and rechecked that he hadn't left anything behind him. He didn't have much to take. The family bible his mother had, some bedding, a change of clothes, his savings, a knife and his gun. Most importantly of all, Granny's ring. He'd made himself a small pouch to wear around his neck and he kept it there.

"Come on boy, let's get out of here in case he comes home early."

Sam, his dog, barked before almost tripping David up by running around his legs. Sam didn't like David's pa either having been a victim of his drunken rage on more than one occasion.

"You excited?" David patted the dog's head. He'd found him half dead a year or two ago. He had fed and looked after him until he had completely recovered. Sam had followed him everywhere since. There was no question of the dog not making the trip to Oregon with him. "I guess you don't feel bad leaving this place," David chatted to the dog as they made their way to the central meeting point. "Neither do I, apart from saying goodbye to Granny."

The wagon train was leaving the next morning, but David had volunteered to help watch the Long's wagon and belongings overnight. Mr. Long told him he was very kind but there was nothing kind about it. If he stayed home, his pa might find out his plans. It would be just his luck for his pa to come home sober.

Granny Thompson had told him to make his peace with his pa before he left but he couldn't do it. He hated the man. His drinking had destroyed David's life. If his pa hadn't been drunk, maybe he'd have found a doctor instead of leaving Ma to birth a baby by herself. He hadn't even helped dig the grave for his wife and newborn daughter. David and his elder brother, Frank, had done it. The next day, Frank took off, and he hadn't seen or heard from him since.

He'd asked Granny to tell Frank where he was if his brother ever came home but had made her promise not to tell his pa. He was done with that man.

* * *

SAM STARTED GROWLING AS SOON as they reached the collection of wagons. David looked up in time to see Harold aim a kick at the dog.

"I wouldn't do that if I were you," he said calmly.

"Why? Are you going to stop me?" Harold laughed.

"Nope. But Sam might just tear your leg off." David smiled as Harold's face lost all color. He whistled to Sam and they walked on toward the Long wagon.

"You best keep that beast under control. Captain Jones won't take kindly to having savages on his train. He's particular about the company he keeps," Harold shouted once there was a safe distance between him and the dog.

"Really? He let you come along, didn't he?" David didn't wait for a reply. He knew he shouldn't goad Harold Chapman. There was little point making enemies of people—not that Harold was his friend. He was another one who had decided years ago that David was as worthless as his pa.

* * *

AT 6 AM the next morning, the bugle sounded. Out on the trail, it would be gunshots from the night watchman at 4 am to wake everyone up, but Captain Jones hadn't wanted to alarm the town residents. He also decided to let them sleep in on the first day. Mrs. Long had breakfast made when David got dressed. She was a good cook and generous too. He ate his fill of pancakes and bacon while listening to the Long children squabble over what chores they had to do. The Long family was just what David had always wanted for himself. Mr. Long clearly adored his wife and judging by her blushes she returned his feelings. Their teenage daughters were pretty and generally well behaved. He smiled to himself at the idea of Eva being jealous of the Long girls. She had no reason to be. He had never looked at another woman. Not since he'd decided in second grade he was going to marry Eva Thompson when he grew up.

He drank back his coffee before thanking Mrs. Long and getting to his feet. It was time for him to start his chores. He'd noticed Mrs. Long slipping Sam his breakfast. Mr. Long hadn't been so keen on the dog at first, but Mrs. Long had persuaded him he would make an excellent guard dog. Sam was taking her seriously. He didn't let the girls out of his sight which was a good thing as the youngest, Julia, was only eight and inclined to wander off. David didn't want to think of the dangers she could face if she tried to explore the camp trails.

Like Mr. Thompson, Mr. Long had decided to use oxen to draw his wagon. David helped Mr. Long hitch up the oxen while the girls went to milk the cows. They had sold off their farm animals save two cows which were making the journey with them. Mrs. Long insisted her girls needed fresh milk every day.

David spotted the Thompson's wagon some way behind the Long's but he made no move to go near it. He didn't know if Mr. Thompson knew he was traveling with the train, and it was best not to annoy Eva's pa if he could avoid it. He'd find out soon enough and with any luck there would be little he could do about it.

Soon the bugle sounded again. It was time to be off. A couple of the townsfolk stood watching as the wagon train rolled out. David caught sight of Granny Thompson—a stray tear trickling down her cheek—as she watched her family move out. He wished he had a way to bring the old lady with them but there was nothing he could do. At her age, the trip was far too dangerous. He looked down at his feet encased in the sturdy boots she'd given him. He had called to her home last night to say goodbye but had been too overcome to say anything, even when she'd leaned up to kiss his cheek. "I hope I am still alive when you and my granddaughter eventually wed. You look after her, mind you or, I will haunt you for the rest of your life."

CHAPTER 12

*J*ohanna held Eva's hand so tightly it hurt but she didn't mind. Anything to distract her from the pain of leaving Virgil. She had clung to Granny until the old woman pushed her away. "Get a hold of yourself, young lady. Remember who you are and where you came from. The Irish have a history of being strong fighting folk, men and women. No more tears."

Eva had struggled as she tried to comply with the request. She wiped away the few tears rolling down her face. "I love you, Granny. I will write to you."

"You better," Granny replied. She wasn't saying much. Eva wondered if she, too, was fighting back the tears despite the lecture.

Johanna, Becky and Ma all hugged Granny as they said goodbye. Stephen held out his hand but at the last minute gave his granny a hug too. They all left Pa to say a private goodbye to the mother he adored.

A couple of their neighbors who weren't making the trek had come to wave them off. Eva saw a couple of men rub their eyes when they thought nobody was looking.

"I hate Pa. And I hate Oregon," she said.

"Stop it, Eva. We have to make the best of things now. You heard what Granny said. Every cloud has a silver lining. We just have to look harder to find it this time." Johanna gave Eva a hug before making her way to the wagon. Pa had sold their farm and some other family would sleep in their loft tonight. Even if Pa decided he wanted to stay, they couldn't change their minds now.

"Pa, look at Harold's wagon. He has his oxen the wrong way round." Stephen was pointing and laughing at the same time.

"Stephen Thompson, behave yourself. I am sure Harold knows what he is doing." Ma didn't sound too confident as she watched Harold trying to get his wagon to move.

"He's got the wheelers at the front and the pointers at the back."

At Ma's empty look, Stephen explained. "You got to put the biggest and strongest nearest the wagon wheels and then the other two at the front. That's how they got their names. I'm right, Pa, ain't I?"

"Yes, Son, but it would be nicer if you were to go offer your help to Harold rather than laughing at him. We are all new to this and we will all make mistakes."

"Sorry, Pa. I didn't intend being mean."

"I know you didn't, Son." Pa jostled her brother's hair but Eva saw the look he exchanged with her ma. She was pleased to see David and Mr. Long hadn't made the same mistake.

"Pa, do you think I should tell him he had to lead from the left and what the commands mean?"

"I think he will work that out for himself, Stephen. Off you go now."

Pa waited until his son had run off before letting himself laugh. "That boy of ours is real smart isn't he, Della?"

"Yes, he inherited your looks and my brains," Ma responded, earning herself a pat on the backside from her husband.

Eva was relieved to see her parents in such a loving, playful mood. After the long months of arguments and bad feelings, it was nice to see them back to their old ways. Even if they were on their way to hated Oregon.

* * *

The first day's travel passed off uneventfully. The wagon train moved along quite slowly but David guessed the captain had decided to let everyone get used to things. It was very different driving a wagon led by oxen compared to one led by horses. The Longs were traveling to the rear of the train. When the ground was dry, the amount of dust the wagons in front would generate made David glad the captain had insisted on rotating the wagons.

He didn't think it fair for anyone to travel at the rear all the time.

He spent some time walking alongside the wagon listening to Mr. Long shouting commands at the oxen. Mr. Long used the bull whip to flick flies away and to direct the oxen but David hadn't seen him hit the oxen. Not like Harold who had cracked it across the backs of his animals more than once. David scowled at the thought and was thankful Captain Jones happened to see Harold in action and had chewed him out over it.

At around noon the signal went out for the wagons to stop and rest for a bit. Captain Jones picked a spot near Bear Creek, which was perfect. The men released the oxen but kept them yoked while the women prepared coffee and leftovers from breakfast. The Long children, who had gone for a nap in the wagon earlier, woke up. They raced off to play with their friends. David decided to go for a walk leaving Mrs. Long writing in her diary. Mr. Long had gone to find some friend in a wagon up ahead.

David walked toward the stream hoping Eva would be there. She was but so was most of her family so he couldn't risk going over to join her. He had to content himself with a smile as she caught sight of him. He wished he knew how to bring her pa around to the idea of their courting.

* * *

"My legs can't walk another step," Johanna said as she walked alongside Eva. Thankfully, Captain Jones gave the order to stop for the night. He told them the wagons had to be parked in a circle. He was very accurate with his calculations and it didn't take long for all the wagons to make a big circle.

"He's doing that to keep the Indians out."

"Stop it, Stephen. There aren't Indians around here," Ma said, although her voice didn't sound too confident. "Make yourself useful and help set up the wall tent. That's where the girls will be sleeping tonight, you can sleep in the wagon."

"Aw, do I have to, Ma? I want to sleep in the open."

"When it's freezing cold in the middle of the night, that won't seem attractive. Now do I have to ask you again?"

"No, Ma'am."

Eva had to turn her head away so nobody saw her smiling at her brother's antics. She couldn't really blame him. He was excited.

Ma and Pa were going to sleep under the wagon. Eva didn't know which would be more comfortable. Being squashed inside the wagon or lying on the ground. At least it was dry. She didn't want to think about camping in the rain.

Pa unyoked the oxen and lead them to the water. Ma started preparing dinner. They would be having a treat tonight as Ma had hidden a pie in the wagon. Eva watched as her ma dug a little trench before adding a few twigs and branches. She got a fire going in no time. Some of the women in the other wagons were struggling to light theirs.

"Ma, maybe you should go help them. I can look after dinner."

"You're a good girl, Eva. Thinking of others like you do."

Ma stood up and went to help the ladies nearest her. Eva set about heating the stew they had made last night. She added some cornbread and beans. It would be tasty and nutritious. She wondered what David would be eating, although he had mentioned Mrs. Long was a good cook. Becky and Johanna were out collecting firewood, at least that is what they had told Ma. Eva suspected Becky was interested in the other people, make that men, traveling with the wagon train. Johanna was probably working out how she could help look after the younger children. She'd mentioned earlier how all the walking would be tough going for them. Her sister had a kind heart, but she often took on so many problems it dragged her down too. Eva hoped she would meet a nice man either on the trail or in Oregon. So far, she had never paid any attention to the opposite sex. Becky did quite enough of that for all of them.

CHAPTER 13

"We travelled eighteen miles today I reckon." Pa refilled his coffee cup.

"It's real pretty countryside. If it's like this the whole way it won't be too bad," Johanna said in a bright voice.

Eva caught the look her parents exchanged but she didn't comment. Everyone was trying to put on a brave face on their journey and she wasn't about to ruin it.

Thank goodness they had listened to Captain Jones and invested in sturdy, well-fitting boots which they wore with good socks. Some of the ladies with the train had taken to walking barefoot—it being preferable to having to deal with blisters caused by the wrong shoes.

Within a week of leaving Virgil, they had made good time and arrived at Quincy. Pa had paid for them to cross the majestic Mississippi in a large steam ferry boat.

"I wish we could take a boat all the way to Oregon. It

RACHEL WESSON

would be so much more comfortable," Becky said wistfully as they all relaxed on deck.

"How's a boat going to cross land and mountains. You girls are all the same—silly," Stephen replied, his tone illustrating what he thought of them.

Eva had to smile at her brother's antics. He hadn't grown out of his excitement over their trip and a week in the wagon hadn't dulled his smile.

"Look, Eva, they got black men doing work on the farm."

"Stop staring, Stephen," Eva said automatically, although her own gaze was focused on the sad looking men.

"Ain't never seen a black man before. What color blood do they have?"

"Now who is being silly? It's red same as ours." Eva's reply sounded harsher than she meant. The sight of grown men looking so miserable was upsetting.

"Do you think we could talk to one?" Stephen wasn't about to be put off.

"Don't see why not if we camp near to their farm," Becky said.

"No, we can't. We will only get them in trouble." Johanna pointed at a white man holding a whip. Eva distracted Stephen. She didn't want to answer any questions about why the man wasn't working and the reason for the whip.

* * *

WHEN THEY CAMPED THAT EVENING, Pa invited the white farmer to sit by their fire. He had come into camp selling eggs and chickens. Pa brought a few chickens and Ma cooked up a feast with the fresh eggs. Eva poured coffee while listening to the men talking.

"He's disgusting. How dare he speak so carelessly about owning human beings."

"Hush, Joanna. He'll hear you," Eva whispered.

"He should hear me. Nobody has the right to sell another human being."

Eva suggested they take a walk. Although her Pa disagreed with slavery he would not want one of his girls showing disrespect to someone invited to share their fire.

"That man should be shot." Johanna's voice trembled making Eva pull her closer.

"Don't upset yourself, Jo, you can't change the whole world."

"How dare he talk like that. He was boasting about how he raised them himself like as if they were calves."

Eva tried to comfort her sister but she was too agitated.

"Imagine, complaining they were only worth one thousand dollars each. He looked so proud of himself when he said he was going to get more work out of them before selling them off for more, I wanted to be sick." Johanna's voice trembled as her body shook. Eva gave her a hug.

"I know. It's horrible but, at least, after tonight we won't have to deal with him again."

David was whittling wood at the Long caravan. The girls stopped to speak to him. Eva watched his expression change from disbelief to anger as Johanna told him about the conversation at the fire. Mrs. Long had come out of her wagon and overheard part of the conversation.

"Those poor people treated worse than pigs fattened up for market. They looked half-starved too." Mrs. Long's eyes glistened.

Eva and David exchanged a look. Her heart beating faster as she guessed what David was about to do. She tried to take his arm, intent on talking him out of it, but one look stopped her.

"Maybe we can do something. Johanna, Eva, get a sack and ask your ma for some leftovers. Don't explain what it's for unless you think she will agree with us. Mrs. Long, do you have any food you can spare?"

"David, don't be taking any risks. The laws in these parts may not be so forgiving," Mrs. Long said, concern etched all over her face.

"Some laws are meant to be broken," David replied gritting his teeth. He packed a sackful of food. Mrs. Long contributed some biscuits and some cooked chicken. He rode back to the farm deciding along the way he would claim he was looking to trade if anyone asked him what he wanted. Nobody challenged him. He made his way into what looked like a barn. There he found the men chained up. It took every ounce of restraint not to take out his gun and shoot the chains off.

Instead, he asked who was their leader. A young man identified himself as Simon. David gave him the food and water apologizing that it wasn't more.

"Someday my friend, I will get my freedom and come to thank you in person," Simon said, his voice gravelly from lack of water.

"There is no need."

"There is every need. You are the first white man to see us as men and not animals. What is your name and where you going?"

"David Clarke. Oregon. We hope to find land to farm."

"Thank you, David." Simon held out his hand. David shook it before murmuring a quick goodbye. He crept back to where he had left his horse and quickly, but quietly, returned to camp.

CHAPTER 14

At first, the weather was fine, but a number of the roads were almost impassable which slowed them down. Then a cold northwest wind made traveling in the wagon particularly uncomfortable, so the sisters walked in a bid to keep warm. Pa and some of the men shot pheasants and some squirrels so they ate well. But lack of water was a big issue, not only for them but for their livestock too. Although there were plenty of streams, the water was so full of mud it was nearly impossible to boil.

Captain Jones told them they would be camping on the bank of the river for two days. The ladies were grateful for a chance to catch up on washing as well as bathing. They teased each other about how dirty they were.

"The mud gets in places where it should never be," Becky moaned one day.

"Where?" asked Stephen curiously.

"Never you mind," Becky replied, trying not to laugh.

Eva was desperate to see David. She hadn't seen him for days. The endless drudgery of the trail was taking its toll on her family. Ma, Becky and herself were short tempered. Only Johanna seemed oblivious to the rough conditions they were traveling under.

Eva was having nightmares about Harold Chapman who made every excuse to see her on the pretext of visiting her pa. If she wasn't dreaming of him, she was thinking of the Donner party and how those poor people suffered. She knew Captain Jones was reliable but even he couldn't control the weather.

* * *

SHE SPOTTED David making his way toward the stream and followed him. He grinned as he heard her approach.

"Captain Jones said we will cross this tomorrow. It looks dangerous."

"We are taking a small ferry. It will be fine."

Eva looked at the boat David pointed to. It was a crazy looking ferry boat. It looked as if it would sink if someone blew hard on it—never mind loaded with a wagon and oxen. Her anxiety must have shown on her face as David put his arms around her shoulders. "Trust me, Eva, it will be safe."

Eva's fear disappeared as David held her close. He pushed her hair back behind her ear, the feel of his fingers making her shiver. She could hear his breathing, slow and steady just like his heartbeat.

His hands brushed the back of her neck before cupping her face. He gazed into her eyes, his thumb gently trailing the outline of her mouth. He bent his head, his lips brushing her cheek as they made their way to her mouth. She trembled in his arms, and he responded by pulling her closer before claiming her mouth with his.

He kissed her gently at first but she wanted more. She wrapped her hands in his coat pulling him closer, groaning softly as he deepened the kiss. She ceased to think about anything but him. Running her fingers down his arms, his muscles taut, as his breathing quickened. He released her mouth, gathered her closer and kissed her forehead.

* * *

SHE TRAILED her mouth across his jawline, the stubble on his chin tickling her skin. His breathing grew ragged as she stroked the side of his face as she kissed every inch of exposed skin above his shirt line. He moaned as her mouth lingered at the hollow in his neck.

"Eva, don't. I can't...we can't..." He rasped.

He held her until both their breathing slowed down. She smiled as he looked down at her. He kissed the freckles on her nose before tracing the outline of her face. "You are so beautiful. So precious."

She leaned against his chest, listening to his heart,

wishing they didn't have to part. She looked up at the sky, the bright stars shining so vividly.

"They are so pretty out here on the prairies," she said softly but David was too intent on kissing her ear to listen. She tried to concentrate on the stars but his kisses were giving her butterflies. She moved so her mouth connected with his. He tasted so good.

After a little while, she broke their kiss.

"I have to go," she said reluctantly. "Pa will be back soon and if he finds me gone..."

He kissed her hard before letting her go. "We belong together, Eva, never forget that. Now go, before you completely bewitch me." His smile was so tender, his expression so full of love, her heart nearly somersaulted.

She walked quickly back to her wagon, knowing without turning back he was watching her. Protecting her just like he always did.

* * *

David stood at the tree watching Eva until she was safely back at her wagon. She was the most amazing girl. Stubborn, strong willed, quick tempered, kind, hardworking and loyal all wrapped up together. Life with her would never be boring. That is if they got a chance to live together. David saw Mr. Thompson in deep conversation with another man, walking back toward his wagon. Eva was safely inside the tent but who was Thompson talking to? The closer the men came, the clearer the vision.

Thompson was shaking Harold's hand. David's heart thudded loudly as he broke out in a sweat. Please God don't let them have agreed to a wedding date. If he was a real man he would march over to Mr. Thompson and demand he allow Eva to marry him. But he had promised Eva not to do anything yet. It was hard keeping his word.

CHAPTER 15

The next few days led them to a splendid looking prairie.

"It looks like a painting doesn't it, Eva?" Becky said while looking around her.

"It surely does," Eva replied taking in the blue-tinged trees in the distance. "So peaceful with all those animal grazing on the land. We could pick some flowers for Ma, it would help cheer her up."

"We should pick some for Pa too. He's still angry at the farmer who tried to charge us ten dollars for grazing the livestock on the prairie. Luckily, he read that guide so he knew what a sharper was."

Eva laughed at the thought of their pa holding flowers. As they made their way back from collecting firewood, Harold stopped them.

"Good afternoon, ladies. Eva, I don't think you should

be collecting firewood. Why don't you pay someone to do it for you?"

Becky let a rather large piece of firewood drop on his foot, earning her a glare in return. "What should she be doing while we're all working?"

"Ignore him, Becky, he has some strange ideas." Eva swept past both of them, carrying the wood toward her ma's fire. How dare he make suggestions about what she should and shouldn't be doing?

"What's got you in a bad mood?" Johanna asked.

"Nothing. Everything."

"She just had another run in with Harold. I wish he had stayed in Virgil," Becky said laying her firewood on top of Eva's.

Eva looked at Johanna, who was smiling and humming a tune.

"Doesn't the mud and traveling affect you Johanna?"

"Sure it does, Eva, but there is no point in getting upset over it. There will be plenty of it on the trail. Captain Jones said when the wind blows a certain way, the dust will make it so we won't be able to see the wagon beside us."

"Hmph." Eva was getting heartily sick of all the things Captain Jones said. It seemed as if everyone was repeating what the captain said. Captain Jones said this and Captain Jones said that.

"Eva, we are going to Oregon. You've got to accept that and stop being such a misery guts. You are making life more uncomfortable than it needs to be."

Johanna never gave lectures. She was always too worried about hurting other people's feelings. She must have behaved very badly for Johanna to act out of character.

"Jo, I'm sorry. I shouldn't moan."

"No, you shouldn't, but you have stopped now. Seriously, Eva, if you saw what some people have to put up with on this trail, you would see we have it easier than most." Jo turned to go back to their wagon leaving Eva to walk alone.

Eva knew her sister meant well but she didn't need to be told to count her blessings. Not today. Eva had intended on going for a long walk to shed a few tears in private but a cry from another wagon got her attention. She made her way over to where a woman was sucking her finger.

"I heard you cry out," she said, wondering if she should have ignored the woman and kept on walking.

"Sorry about that. I cut my finger trying to peel potatoes." The woman looked at the pile of potatoes beside her. "I told Stan I wasn't cut out for this trek but he wouldn't listen."

Eva felt sorry for the woman despite the fact her clothes and wagon were of a much better quality than her family's.

"Can I help? It can be a bit tricky cooking outside when you are not used to it," Eva asked, hoping she wouldn't insult the other woman.

"Would you mind? Don't you have your own family to see to?"

"No. Ma has plenty of help. My name's Eva."

"Amelia but my friends call me Milly."

Eva took the job of peeling the potatoes. Amelia was wasting so much food as she kept cutting the peels off in chunks. "Why don't you chop the onions and I will do the potatoes. So where are you from?"

"Boston."

"Wow, you have come a long way. I've never been to a big city. What's it like?" Eva was always curious about faraway places.

"Well, some will tell you it's noisy and overcrowded. It certainly does seem that way after seeing all this." Milly looked around at the wide-open grasslands. "But I think it's wonderful. For one thing, the stores have cooked food so I wouldn't have to eat another burnt offering again."

Eva smiled, sensing the girl was lonely and needed to talk.

"Mother and Father have a lovely house. I guess I didn't realize how lucky I was growing up the way I did. I didn't even know how some people lived but I think I have seen everything now." Milly bit her lip.

Eva tried her best to distract her. "What made you decide to go to Oregon?"

"Stan wanted to go. I'm his wife so where he goes, I go."

"But surely you talked about it. Didn't you tell him you wanted to stay in Boston?" Eva knew her question was rather intrusive given she had just met Milly but she couldn't help wondering why a husband would force someone like Milly to move so far from home.

"Stan kept talking about how wonderful it would be. Stan is, I mean was a lawyer. He has a way with words. But now he wants to become a farmer." Milly took several deep breaths. "I don't know the first thing about farming."

Eva saw the tears glistening in the other girl's eyes. She figured the trail was all too much for her.

It was people like this Johanna had been talking about earlier. Looking around, it was obvious Milly hadn't the first idea about making a home on the range. She had little to no firewood and there wasn't any sign of any preparations for the next morning's breakfast. Her wagon seemed well stocked but stores of raw food never helped anyone's mood. No wonder the girl was in tears.

"Milly, why don't you and your husband come and eat at our fire tonight? Ma loves meeting new people, and I know she would be fascinated to hear more about Boston. Pa would enjoy talking to your husband as he likes educated men."

"I don't know. What would your mother say to two more people just turning up? Stan eats a lot even if all I manage to cook is usually burnt." Milly smiled self-consciously.

"Ma won't mind. I will go tell her now. Then I will come back with Johanna, she's my younger sister. She is much better at organizing a kitchen—indoor or outdoor than I am. Together we will get you more organized."

"I can't believe you are helping me like this. You are so kind."

"Not really. I was dreading the journey. Now I have someone to talk to, the time will go much quicker. I am quite selfish after all," Eva said before she left to speak to her ma.

Ma didn't mind having guests for dinner, although she complained a little about the short notice.

"Good thing I made fresh bread, it will help the food go further," she said tutting as she worked out her menu.

"I'm sorry, Ma, but I just felt so sorry for her. Stephen would make a better job of peeling the potatoes. She obviously has never had to fend for herself before. The poor girl is really overwhelmed."

"Don't apologize, Eva, it was a nice thing you did. You and Johanna go back and try to help your friend get organized. Becky will help me here."

Becky muttered something but soon shut up when Ma's gaze landed on her.

"Thanks for coming back with me, Johanna. I know you are better at homemaking than me," Eva said as the two sisters picked their way through the muddy patches toward Milly's wagon.

"I just paid a bit more attention to Ma that's all."

"You were right earlier. Some people really do have a hard time on the trail."

"No matter what our troubles are, there are always those worse off," Johanna said with a pious expression on her face.

Eva hit her gently on the arm. "Stop teasing. I know I was whining earlier but I am over it now."

* * *

THE TWO SISTERS helped Milly get organized. Eva collected some twigs and wood for her fire. Johanna showed her how to make dough for bread. "You can leave that rising now. Cook it overnight and it will make a nice treat for your husband during the day."

"Stan will fall over if I make something soft enough to eat." Milly's expression was so funny, both sisters laughed.

"Sorry, we aren't laughing at you but you should see your face. We all had to learn how to do this. You will master it in no time," Eva said kindly.

"I wouldn't place a bet on that. We had a cook and servant. Before we came out here, I never had to go near a stove or wash anything. It's been an eye opener for sure."

They had a lovely dinner that evening. Ma excelled herself as usual. Stan and Milly ate as if they hadn't eaten for days. Stan was extremely thankful for both the invitation to dinner and the fact the girls were helping his wife.

Milly and Johanna carried some leftovers back to Milly's wagon. Eva stayed behind doing the dishes. She overhead Stan speaking to her parents.

"I expected too much of Milly bringing her out here alone. I should have listened to her father, but I thought he was just being overprotective."

"Your wife is young and healthy. She will learn," Pa said in his no nonsense tone.

"What my husband means is we will be happy to help you both as much as we can," Ma added quickly.

"Your daughters have taught her so much already, but I bet it's their company that has brought a real smile to her face."

Eva finished the washing, her thoughts centered on David. What would it be like for them when they married? What if he decided he wanted to live somewhere across the country away from her family? She would have to go with him just as Milly had no choice but to accompany Stan. Maybe marriage wasn't such a bed of roses after all. David would listen to her though. He always treated her as an equal. But you aren't married yet. The little voice in her head persisted despite her best attempts to ignore it.

CHAPTER 16

"Johanna, Pa says we will reach Saint Joseph tomorrow. That will be our last stop in the United States."

"Do you think he will let us go shopping?" Becky wondered.

"Not likely given those clouds in the sky. Captain Jones said bad weather is on its way. He wants to cross the Missouri as soon as possible."

"Since when have you been getting cosy with Captain Jones?" Becky's petulant expression warned Eva a fight was brewing.

"Johanna is repeating what Captain Jones told Pa. He mentioned he would have to collect some provisions he sent down by river. We can't go without them."

"Where is he going to put them? We are already really crowded."

Eva agreed with her sister but her pa was adamant the

journey couldn't be completed without the rest of his stuff. But she had to trust he was being sensible. She had heard him arguing with Harold about taking too much stuff with him. Harold was talking about how much money he would make. He wasn't in the mood for listening to anyone, not Pa and not Captain Jones. Eva had almost clapped when she saw how much Harold had upset Pa. Maybe he would finally see Harold Chapman was not good marriage material.

As Eva suspected they were not able to go shopping in St. Joseph. She was glad as the whole town seemed to be full of men going west. They crossed the river without incident and soon found themselves in the middle of a very pretty valley. There was plenty of grass for their livestock and for once everyone was happy.

Sometime later they met a caravan train moving in the opposite direction. Pa stopped to speak to some of the men. Turned out they had lost so many to disease, they had decided to turn back. Harold rode up and began negotiating with them for their wagon and oxen. Eva listened with her mouth open as he tried to convince the men to part with their wagons.

"You could travel quicker by horseback and the travel across the river to Saint Joseph would be cheaper."

The men looked from Harold to Eva's pa and back. They were so disheartened it looked like they were going to accept Harold's offer.

Eva watched her pa. He wasn't happy. He excused himself and Harold and took the younger man aside. Eva didn't have to listen too hard, her pa's angry words carried on the wind. She smiled as her pa gave Harold a lecture about not taking advantage of people. Her pa named a price that made Harold's face pale. It was quite a bit higher than the amount he had offered. He came back to the travelers and offered them the higher figure. Once they agreed, he stomped off back to his wagon. The captain of the other wagon train came forward to thank Eva's pa for intervening on their behalf.

"Think nothing of it." Pa's face showed his embarrassment.

Eva didn't comment until they were almost back to their own wagon. "I am glad you were there today, Pa. Otherwise, those poor families would have lost out."

Pa didn't say anything. He seemed to be deep in thought. Eva decided not to push the point home. Harold was showing his true colors and it looked like Pa might finally be seeing him for the man he was.

* * *

DAVID WAS REALLY ENJOYING the trip to Oregon. For the first time, people accepted him for who he was rather than who his parents were. Most of the people traveling with Captain Jones hadn't lived in Virgil. The few families who had, treated him really well anyway. Mrs. Freeman had often invited him to their home when he and Joey were in school together. The only person who ever gave him any trouble was Harold Chapman.

While David disliked Harold not only because he was a bully but because of the way he treated the animals in his care, Harold seemed to absolutely hate David. His dislike was so obvious Captain Jones had asked David if there was any history between them. David had replied, "No," which was true unless you took Eva into account. Harold had made his plan to marry Eva quite public. But that was none of David's concern. Eva was free to marry whomever she liked, he just hoped it would be him.

"You have a real way with animals, Clarke. What do you plan on doing in Oregon?" Captain Jones asked him one day when they were out scouting together.

"I want to have a farm. I would love to raise horses but I don't have the money for that. So instead, I will be a farmer."

Captain Jones didn't comment. David wasn't even sure he had heard his answer as the captain's attention was trained on the horizon.

"I wanted to be a farmer once. Maybe I still will," Jones said.

"I don't know how you keep trekking back and forth to Oregon." David wanted the captain to know he wasn't complaining. "I mean I like the traveling but it will be a relief to finally sleep in a real bed in a house that doesn't move in the wind."

Captain Jones smiled. "I have had enough of trekking. This will be my last trip. I don't mind the traveling or the animals. It's the people who bother me."

David burst out laughing thinking the captain was joking but when Jones didn't smile, he stopped.

"You are serious. I thought you were joking."

"No, I'm serious. I'm not talking about the Longs, Freemans or other families like them. But people like Chapman and his friends annoy me. They are so ignorant"

David wasn't sure what Harold had done now, but he wasn't about to defend him. He stayed silent. They rode on for a while until they came upon an area littered with buffalo carcasses.

"Stupid, selfish idiots." Captain Jones' face turned red from anger. "They have no thought for anyone other than themselves."

David didn't know who "they" were.

"They didn't even take the meat but simply butchered them because they could. And they call the Indians the savages."

"Who do?" David couldn't stop himself. He was too curious.

"White men probably from a train ahead of us."

"But how do you know?" David asked again.

"The waste. No Indian, regardless of their tribe, would behave like this. They honor animals only killing those they need. When they kill one buffalo they use every piece of him right down to the bones."

David looked at the field as Captain Jones carried on speaking.

"These animals would have fed an entire village for months. Yet now, they are just lying here wasting away."

"How come you know so much about the Indians?"

At the look on the other man's face, he wondered if he had gone too far.

"Sorry, I am always asking questions. Eva says it is because my mind is too busy."

"Eva? Oh yes, Rebecca Thompson's older sister. Pretty girl."

"Yes, she is. She's special."

"Not as fiery as her younger sister?"

"No, Becky has a hotter temper that's for sure." David confirmed. "But you wouldn't want to cross my Eva either."

"Your Eva? Ah, the girl you mentioned that first day we met."

David blushed at Captain Jones' teasing.

"Well, yes. Hopefully soon, but one day."

"I take it her pa has other ideas?"

"How do you know?" David didn't want to admit Mr. Thompson's feelings about him were public knowledge.

"Becky may have mentioned it once or twice. Very impulsive young lady. Headstrong but rather beautiful."

David looked curiously at the older man. So he wasn't immune to Becky's charms.

"Don't look at me like that. I am far too old to be getting involved with a girl as young as Becky."

"Not too sure you have much of a choice. From my experience, when the Thompson women get an idea in their heads, it's mighty hard to shift it." Then David stopped teasing. "Unless, of course, you mean you are married already."

"I was. Once. Not anymore."

The captain's closed expression warned David not to pry.

"How much longer do you think we will be? My stomach is getting mighty hungry." David's stomach growled as if to confirm his words.

"We should head back. I just want to check the stream up above. If those hunters killed buffalo near it, we won't be able to camp here."

They checked it and thankfully it was clear. Otherwise, they would have had to find a new route to water and that could take hours. They rode back to camp in silence but it wasn't awkward. David had been surprised at how much Jones had spoken today. Usually, he was a man of very few words.

CHAPTER 17

"*E*va, dig the trench will you, please? With this wind blowing, I am never going to get a fire going." Ma turned to her other daughter. "Becky, take Stephen and go and collect some buffalo chips. I am running low."

"Aw, Ma, do we have to? They stink."

"Do you want a hot breakfast? Better yet, why don't you go tell your pa he can't have a decent breakfast because you won't do your chores?"

Eva hid a smile at the mutinous look on her sister's face as she headed out to collect the dung. The mere mention of Pa was usually enough to get any of them moving faster.

"You can take that grin off your face, Eva Thompson. If you had collected enough yesterday, your brother and sister wouldn't be out there now."

"Yes, Ma. Sorry, Ma," Eva repeated, not wanting to annoy her ma any more. She was in a ferocious mood these past few days. The lack of washing facilities, not to mention being able to change into clean clothes, was proving tiresome. Her ma had always prided herself on having a clean family.

"Ma, can you help me, please? The flame won't catch."

"I don't have time to wait today. We are behind enough as it is. Stand back, Eva."

Eva stood back as her ma sprinkled the fuel with a little gun powder. She soon had a nice fire going, though Eva didn't think her Pa would be best pleased if he knew his gunpowder had helped.

With a grin at her ma, she quickly roasted some coffee beans so they could grind them to make fresh coffee. Her ma fried slices of bacon. Then she added a couple of eggs. She made pancakes in the skillet. Eva was impressed. Her ma made everything look so easy.

"Call your Pa will you, please, Eva? He was on late guard duty so deserved a bit of a lie-in this morning. Then can you round up your brother and sister. We don't want to cause the train to be late pulling out."

Eva did as she was bid. By the time she came back with her siblings dragging their feet behind her, Pa had eaten. He was in a good mood.

"We are making good progress. We did the right thing taking this caravan. I knew Captain Jones was the man to follow."

* * *

THE REST of the day passed without incident. Eva had just cleaned up the last of the dinner dishes when she heard a whistle.

"Eva, I think it was for you." Becky gave her a gentle nudge. "Go on."

Glancing quickly in her ma and pa's direction to check they weren't looking, she ran over quickly to where David was standing.

"Can you get away for a little while. I have a surprise for you," he said after kissing her.

"I'm not sure. Pa would have a fit if I went out alone so late."

"It's not dark yet. Please, Eva, come with me. It's important."

Eva looked around but her ma and pa were still chatting to the family in the neighboring wagon.

Becky came nearer. "Go on, Eva, I will keep a watch on the others. If you hear me singing, it means pa and ma are looking for you."

Eva grinned at her sister. Becky's singing was legendary for all the wrong reasons. The girl was beautiful but she didn't have the voice of an angel.

She took David's hand and they walked up a small hill.

"I wanted to do something special for you," he said softly. "I hope you will feel better after seeing it."

Eva appreciated his thoughtful gesture, but she wasn't sure anything could make her feel better. She missed her granny and the family and friends they had left behind. As they climbed the small hill, she held onto her skirts with one hand while holding David's hand tighter with the other. When they reached the top, David let go of her hand and took something out from under his coat.

"It's a spy glass. Mr. Long lent it to me. Look through here."

Eva's skin tingled at his touch as he stood behind her, putting his arms around her as he held the spyglass for her to look through. She could see the city of St. Joseph. It looked so close, she felt she could touch it if she held out her hand.

"Eva, I promise if you don't like Oregon I will bring you back to Saint Joseph one day, and from there we will take whatever is the fastest route back to Virgil." He held her tightly as she sniffed, obviously guessing she was in tears. She looked one last time through the glass before turning into his arms.

"I don't care where I live so long as we are together." She stood on her tippy-toes to kiss him. He held her tighter as their feelings mounted. David broke away first.

"We best get back. Don't want your pa raising the alarm when he discovers you have disappeared."

"David, we will find a way for us to be together, won't we?"

"I promise you, Eva, I will do everything it takes to convince your pa to let us wed." David took her hand and gently led her back down the hill. "The last thing we need is to provoke your pa by giving him a heart attack. We need to hurry."

She picked up her skirt once they reached the summit

and they raced back to the train. Out of breath, she skidded to a halt shortly before reaching her wagon. Thankfully, her pa and ma were still chatting. She waved goodbye to David who had waited at a tree for fear of making her pa angrier, before climbing into the tent she was sharing with her sister.

"You took long enough," Becky complained as soon as Eva lay down.

Eva ignored her sister. She wouldn't understand what it was like to be in love. Eva closed her eyes, determined to dream of her wedding. To David.

CHAPTER 18

The days were long and tiring. They had to balance making good progress with finding grazing for the cattle and livestock. Every day they passed fresh graves along the trail. It was hard not to dwell on the things that could go wrong. Occasionally, they met trains heading in the opposite direction. The travelers having given up on their dream of reaching Oregon or California.

Most people walked having found traveling in the wagon was very uncomfortable no matter how many feather beds they lay on. Captain Jones always made them rest for about two hours at noon. But while the animals and men rested, the women found they had plenty of chores to keep them busy.

* * *

JOHANNA SPAT the dust from her mouth. It got everywhere no matter what precautions they took. The sheer number of wagons on the train meant at times the dust was so thick, they couldn't see.

"Can I take the children down the cut off paths? The constant dust isn't healthy for the little ones. I will stay close to the train." Sensing Captain Jones was going to say no, she pretended to be Becky. Her twin would smile and flirt until she got the answer she wanted. "Please, Captain Jones, don't say no."

He looked at her, before looking at the children around her.

"I assume you know how to shoot?" He asked her quietly obviously not wanting to alarm the younger ones.

"Pa showed me how to use a gun. I couldn't kill anyone," at the frown on his face she quickly continued, "but I can shoot a warning shot to tell you we are in trouble."

"All right but don't wander off too far."

"Thank you."

Johanna gathered the children together and told them they were going to take a new route away from the dust. First they had to go tell their parents they were with her. She didn't want any frantic mothers chasing after them.

When the children returned, Johanna took Julia's hand and together they led the children down one of the narrow cut offs. These trails had been used by hunters and sometimes Indians. She watched as the children ran around picking berries and wildflowers for their mothers. It was so pleasant walking when you weren't surrounded by dust.

"Can you sing to us Jo?" Julia asked her after they had been walking for about two hours. Johanna had carried the younger ones for a little while, each one taking turns. The sun was getting high and it would soon be time to return to the wagon train. She started singing Turkey in the Straw. The children joined in, singing and clapping. A loud rustling sound in the bushes stopped everyone. Johanna almost wept at the look of fear on the young children's faces. She put a hand over the gun in her pocket. She couldn't shoot anyone but it didn't stop her for being thankful she had taken it. Almanzo Price, a nine year old boy, took a knife from his pocket.

"You stay back. I will protect you."

"Put the knife away Almanzo."

"But I am the only man of the group."

Johanna bent down to his level. She put an arm on his shoulder. "Can you protect the girls while I go look in the bushes? You need to be very brave." The boy stood straighter and looked her in the eye although he couldn't stop his hands from shaking. "Yes Ma'am. Be careful and call me if you need me."

Johanna nodded gravely.

Taking deep breaths she moved toward the bushes her mind telling her if it had been Indians they would have attacked already. The rustling grew louder as did her heart beats. She picked up a stick and used it to poke at the bush. She gasped before laughing aloud at the sight in front of her. A very content ox was chomping on the leaves of the bush.

"What is it Jo?" The children asked coming closer.

"It's an ox. Someone must have lost him."

"Can we keep him? He looks like a nice one," Julia asked putting out her hand to stroke his moist snout.

"He may follow us back to camp Julia but I think he might prefer to stay here and eat. Speaking of lunch, we need to get back to the wagon train," Johanna smoothed down her dress. "Let's get back before they send scouts out looking for us."

She was relieved to see Almanzo had sheathed his knife.

"I'm glad it wasn't an Indian. I don't feel like killing anything today."

"Killing is wrong, Almanzo."

"But Indians deserve it. Pa said so," Almanzo said, a fierce expression on his face.

"Nobody deserves to be killed," Johanna responded firmly.

* * *

THEY RETURNED to the wagon trains, the children running ahead anxious to tell their parents what had happened with the ox. Johanna returned to her Pa's wagon. There she met Eva and Becky. She saw their glance of concern when she didn't greet them. Usually she was cheerful but Almanzo's comment had upset her. Why would any parent teach a child it was a good thing to kill another person? She couldn't understand that thinking at all. If she ever had children, they would be brought up to respect everyone regardless of skin color, nationality or religion.

* * *

"I WISH ma would let us wear bloomers. I am sick of the rocks giving me bumps and bruises." Becky complained as they got dressed for bed one night.

Johanna felt her pain. Their Ma had suggested sewing small rocks into the hems of their dresses in order to stop the wind from whipping up their skirts and robbing them of their modesty. They may have been saved the embarrassment of revealing their underthings to the male members of the train but were their bruised and blackened shins worth it?

"At least we don't have to do the chores we did at home. I hated churning butter." Becky rubbed her arms as if remembering the aching muscles.

"Ma came up with a good idea for butter, didn't she?" Johanna said. "By leaving the milk in the churn at the back of the wagon, the butter makes itself."

"See, you can always find the bright side. The continuous bumps along this trail are good for something if only for shaking milk." Becky's sarcastic reply didn't stop Johanna.

"Becky, there are many good things about the trail. You are meeting lots of new people," Johanna reminded her sleepily.

Becky sat up in the tent. "Captain Jones is dreamy, don't you think?"

"Captain Jones is too old for you," Johanna said firmly.

"Why? Older men marry young women all the time. At least with him, I wouldn't have to settle down into the boring life of a home maker," Becky said dreamily.

"No, you would be too busy moaning about trekking across the country twice a year. That's if he brought you with him. I think he would be more likely to leave you behind at home with the children." Johanna's tone was even firmer than before.

"What's got into you, Johanna?" Eva asked her sister gently. "I'm normally the one throwing water on Becky's wilder ideas." Eva was concerned about the younger twin. She had been in a funny mood all day. Something was bothering her.

"Nothing. I am just tired. Good night." Johanna lay down again and pulled the covers up over her ears. Becky and Eva exchanged looks. For all Becky's wild ideas and willful ways, she genuinely cared for her twin.

"Get some sleep, Becky. It's late."

Eva lay back down but sleep wouldn't come. It had been a difficult day. Some people were feeling very ill. David said it was the bad water. It sure didn't taste nice.

Ma insisted they all, including Stephen, drink coffee rather than the water. She made them sieve the water before putting it on to boil. It was rather disgusting what they found floating in it. Dead flies and other insects made Eva's stomach roil.

CHAPTER 19

*T*hey were woken early by the bugle sounding a cry of alarm. Becky ran out of their tent without her wrap. She came running back. "Ma says a child has gone missing. We're to get dressed and help in the hunt.

"Who is it?" Johanna asked, fear making her voice tremble.

"Julia Long."

Eva's heart lurched. That was the girl whose family David was working with. She dressed quickly determined to find her. Running toward their wagon she saw David in the distance. She picked up her skirts and ran to him. "Any news?"

David shook his head gravely. "We don't know how long she's been gone. One of her sisters woke up and found her missing. Maybe she's sleepwalking?"

They both looked around but saw nothing but acres of grass and Johanna running towards them.

"Where's Sam?" She asked looking for David's dog.

"He's off chasing prairie dogs. Why?"

"He's gone after Julia. You know he never lets her out of his sight. I bet he's gone to find her."

"Miss Thompson, I know you think highly of animals but Sam is just a dog. He ain't been trained in nothing." David dismissed Jo's suggestion.

"Dog's know how to protect. It's part of their nature. Find Sam and you will find Julia," Johanna insisted.

Eva looked at David who shrugged his shoulders.

"Might as well give it a try. Nobody has had any better ideas," Eva said.

The three of them headed in the direction of where David had seen Sam go. They spread out a bit to cover more ground.

"Mind for gopher holes and rattlesnakes. I don't want to have to take either of you back to your pa with a twisted ankle or a snake bite."

"We will be careful." Johanna called back, her gaze centered on the horizon. "Sam, come here. Sam." She called, listening for an answer but they heard nothing.

They walked for about an hour before stopping. The sun had come out and it was very warm. They were all thirsty. David wanted Eva and Johanna to turn back. "Your pa is going to flay me alive for letting you wander so far from the wagon train."

"You didn't let us. We were going regardless," Eva insisted.

"Shush you two. Listen." Johanna looked into the distance as if she had heard something.

Eva and David listened but heard nothing. Johanna shouted to Sam. They listened again and then it came. They heard a dog barking excitedly. Sam ran toward them, ran around them, and then ran back in the direction he had come.

David ran in the direction of the noise with Johanna and Eva following as close behind him as their skirts allowed.

David came to a sudden stop holding out his arms to prevent the two sisters from getting any closer.

"Sam's got Julia but look." David spoke quietly as he pointed at the girl.

The girls looked at the dog who was lying on the ground next to a sleeping Julia. Johanna took a step forward, but Sam growled making her move back.

"Why is Sam growling at me?"

"Didn't you see it? It's coiled up on the rock beside Julia's leg," David whispered.

Eva stared at the horrible sight. She hated snakes of any kind, even the harmless ones. But rattlesnakes gave her nightmares.

"What are we going to do?" she squeaked.

"You girls are going to stand right there. You cannot make a sound. We don't want anything to antagonize the snake. They are quite harmless unless provoked."

Eva had always thought she would believe anything David said but not this time. A snake was never harmless.

"What are you going to do?" She asked, feeling as if her heart was in her throat.

"I have to either get rid of the snake before Julia wakes up, or get her out quickly. If she moves suddenly..."

David took a step toward Sam who whimpered.

"See, he's worried about David. Dogs are intelligent creatures." Johanna whispered to Eva but she couldn't respond.

Her eyes were glued to the snake. David continued to move slowly. He unsheathed his bowie knife, the silver blade glinting in the strong sunlight. Ma will kill us for coming out without our bonnets. Eva couldn't believe she had just thought of bonnets now. At a time like this. She started to pray as she watched David, unable to breathe.

"Shush, Sam, good boy."

The girls heard David murmuring to the dog who stared back at him but didn't move. David continued to move slowly.

Johanna poked Eva in the side. "Julia's waking up. Oh, please God, let her stay still. I can't watch." Johanna curled her head into Eva's shoulder. She couldn't move, not even to put her hand around her.

David moved quicker than she had ever seen anyone move before. She saw the sun glint off the knife and then a rattling sound. She tried to take a step but she couldn't move. Sam was barking like crazy.

"I can't look." Johanna mumbled. Eva gave her sister's hand a quick squeeze.

"David's fine. He's carrying Julia," Eva quickly reassured Johanna.

"She's fine. A bit shocked and dehydrated but she will be alright," David said.

Eva held out her arms to give the little girl a cuddle. "I want my ma." The tear-streaked face looking up at her, made Eva's heart turn over.

"We will take you back to your ma now, darling. She's been worried about you."

"Is she angry?" The poor child was terrified.

"No, darling, she will be really happy to see you home," Eva quickly reassured the child.

David carried Julia while Johanna gave Sam lots of hugs.

"You're my hero, Sam." Johanna kissed the dog's head.

Sam barked and jumped up on her before racing around them barking the entire time.

Eva gave David a quick kiss over Julia's head. "Are you alright? You weren't bitten, were you?"

"No, but only thanks to your granny." He held out his foot pointing at his boot.

Bile rose in Eva's mouth at the sight of two small dents in the leather.

"Thank God granny got them for you," Johanna said smiling at him. "She obviously approves of your plan to marry my sister."

With that Johanna walked toward the wagons with Sam circling between her and David.

"How does she know I want to marry you? I thought

that was a secret," David asked, a bemused expression on his face.

"It is or, at least, it should be. But Johanna is different than the others. She always seems to know things she shouldn't. She won't say anything, don't worry," Eva said quietly not wanting Julia to repeat anything to her parents.

"I am not worried. Today is further proof we never know what will happen. I wish I could speak to your pa."

"I do too, David, but he won't listen. Give him time."

David looked at her as if to ask how much time does he need but he didn't say anything. He shuffled Julia to a more comfortable position and started walking back to the wagons.

Eva walked beside David, thanking God for him and Granny. She had come so close to losing him. Few people recovered from snake bites at home in Virgil. Never mind out here in the middle of nowhere. More than anything, Eva wanted to turn around and head home. Back to Virgil. To her granny and the safety of their town. There was nice food and clean water and few snakes.

CHAPTER 20

s they got nearer to the caravan train, Mrs. Long came running, holding her skirts up around her ankles. "My baby!" she screamed. "Is she de...hurt?"

"No, Mrs. Long. She just needs a cuddle and something to eat and drink," David said, his tone reassuring as the woman drew closer.

"Thanks to Sam and David," Johanna added.

"Sam?" Mrs. Long took her child from David as Mr. Long came running.

"Sam found her and stayed with her until we arrived. Johanna, I mean Miss Thompson, had the bright idea of tracking Sam as she believed he would be with Julia. She was right."

Johanna backed away from the crowd. Eva knew her sister didn't like being the center of attention. Their pa and ma arrived just as Johanna had turned toward their wagon.

"What's going on? Where were you girls? Your mother

was frantic," Pa said, anger making his tone severe.

"Please don't be cross with them. They saved young Julia, with David," Mr. Long replied.

"You were with him?" Pa said crossly.

Eva had to take a couple of deep breaths as she fought her instinct to scream back at her father.

"David saved Julia's life, Pa. There was a rattler sunning itself on a stone near to where she was lying. If David hadn't killed it, well..." Johanna left the rest unsaid.

Eva sent her sister a look of gratitude before checking her father's reaction. He looked stunned and dare she believe it, a little ashamed.

"A rattlesnake. It didn't hurt Julia, did it?" Mrs. Long checked her daughter.

"No, ma'am. Julia is a little sunburnt and got a bad scare," David confirmed.

"It's true, Pa. Look at his boot. The snake left its mark." Stephen crouched down to see David's boot. "Wow, that looks like a big one. How did you kill it? Did you shoot it?"

"Never mind about that. I am sure Mr. Clarke and our girls could do with some coffee and something to eat. Why don't you and your family join us for breakfast, Mr. Long? I will take something to your wife to eat once she sees to Julia. I have some salve to help with her sunburn." Ma quickly took charge.

Eva was relieved. Now that they were all safe, she felt her body tremble. It must be some sort of delayed reaction to the shock.

"Thank ye kindly," Mr. Long replied watching his wife

carry their little one into the wagon. "Thank you, David, and both of you, young ladies, for saving my girl. I don't know what the missus would have done if anything had happened."

Eva saw his eyes glistening just as he turned away. He was probably embarrassed. Men never cried, particularly in front of strangers. Her pa and ma walked back to the wagon deep in conversation. She gave David a quick hug before following them.

* * *

DAVID SOUNDED the signal to let the other men know the danger was over. Captain Jones returned soon afterward with the men from the other search parties.

"How is the girl?" he asked.

"She is much better thanks to Mr. Clarke and my sisters," Becky announced. "You would think she had rescued Julia all by herself." Johanna whispered to Eva who watched as Becky put her arm through Captain Jones' who looked stunned. It was rather amusing to see the confidant captain looking unsure of himself. Becky drew him toward the Long wagon.

"You will see for yourself she is alright. A little burned and, of course, the poor child was awfully scared. When I think of the dangers she faced, I could swoon."

At that last remark, Eva had to turn away for fear of laughing. The idea of Becky swooning over anything was so farfetched it was funny. She was glad she could feel amused. After the events of this morning, she thought she would never feel anything but fear again.

They were allowed a quick breakfast before Captain Jones gave the instruction to move out.

"He could have given us a little more time to get over what happened," Eva moaned, feeling very tired after her long walk combined with the sleepless night.

"We have to make up lost ground. You know we need to be over the mountains before winter closes in. Captain Jones knows what he is doing," Becky snapped.

"Don't bite my head off, Becky. I was just saying."

"Well, don't. We have enough to put up with. We don't need your whining on top of it." Becky marched off leaving Eva staring after her.

"Don't mind her. I heard Captain Jones tell her he wasn't the marrying kind."

"Pa would have a fit if he knew they were talking like that," Eva responded, more than a little shocked. She knew her sister was forward but hadn't realized she was that bad.

"I think he was trying to let her down gently," Johanna said looking after her twin. "Pity it will have the completely opposite effect."

"What do you mean?"

"Eva, I know you think I am totally naïve but even I know Becky always wants what she can't have." Johanna walked on after their sister leaving Eva to trail along behind. It was true what Johanna had said but if Becky thought anyone would agree to a match between her and the captain, she was in for a shock.

CHAPTER 21

"We will arrive at Fort Kearney the day after tomorrow. Can you imagine all those dashing young soldiers? I heard a rumor Captain Jones has agreed to camp there for a couple of nights. There is going to be a dance and everything," Becky said swaying back and forth as if she was dancing.

"What may I ask is everything?"

Becky's face fell. "Sorry, Pa, I didn't know you were there."

"Obviously. You won't be going to any dances. You are far too young."

"But, Pa, I am sixteen, nearly seventeen. You met Ma when she was younger than me."

Eva sneaked a look at her ma and saw her blushing. She waited for Pa's response to Becky, but it seemed his daughter had done something rare and left him speechless.

"Please, Pa. You and Ma will be there to make sure nothing happens. I will only be dancing, not kissing or..."

"Kissing? Who said anything about that? I think you read too many of those trashy dime novels, young lady."

"She didn't mean anything by it, Pa. She's just excited and wants to go to the dance," Eva intervened quickly on her sister's behalf. "We all do. It would be good to have a night away from the trail and the dust and the..."

"Alright, you can go to the dance. I can't fight all the women in my house. But you remember your manners."

Becky threw her arms around Pa nearly knocking him over in the process. "You are the best pa in the whole world."

Eva wasn't looking forward to the dance as she knew her pa wouldn't let her dance with David. The thought of Harold holding her in his arms made her ill. The only light on the horizon was the fact that her pa seemed to be less fond of Harold than he had been at home. Maybe he was seeing him for the person he really was. Captain Jones certainly didn't like him—having told him off more than once—for his treatment of his team as well as the load in his wagon.

"Pa, did you know the army bought the fort from a fur trading company and it hasn't been here that long either?" Stephen said excitedly. He couldn't wait to see the soldiers. He wanted to ask them about the Indians they had fought.

* * *

Eva went down to the stream to rinse out some clothes. Gracie, Becky's friend from Virgil, was already there.

"Eva, did you hear about the dance?"

"Yes, Gracie, Becky was telling Pa all about it at suppertime."

"Won't it be nice to do something other than walking and chores?"

"Yes, I suppose," Eva answered trying for her friend's sake to sound optimistic.

"What's wrong with you? I thought you liked dancing."

"I do, it's just.... Oh, never mind me. I'm tired is all."

Gracie looked at her but Eva wasn't going to tell her friend the real reason. She liked Gracie a lot but she tended to gossip.

"Who are you looking to dance with, Gracie?"

Gracie blushed. "You won't believe me."

"Captain Jones," Eva said joking but then caught the look in her friend's eyes. "Really? You want to dance with the captain? But he is about fifteen years older than you."

"So what. There is a lot to be said for a mature man." Gracie had a dreamy look in her eyes.

Eva sighed. Becky and her best friend were both fascinated by the same man. There was bound to be trouble. "But maybe he is already married."

"He isn't. He told Pa this was likely to be his last train. He wants to claim some of the Oregon land himself."

Funny Eva couldn't see Captain Jones in the role of a farmer. He seemed too...

"And if he gets his land, he'll need someone to set up home with. Won't he?"

"I take it that will be you," Eva said, thinking not if Becky gets to him first. She liked Gracie but next to her sister her friend wouldn't stand a chance.

"Why not? I am old enough to be wed. I know how to run a home. Ma's showed me everything. I can make him a good wife."

"Gracie, I know all that. You will make any man a fantastic wife. I just wondered about the age difference. What will your pa think?" Eva was hoping to put Gracie off. She didn't want her friend getting hurt.

"I think Pa is quite taken with him."

Eva was surprised. She didn't think her own pa would agree to a match with a man so much older.

"Does Joey Freeman know you are interested in Captain Jones?"

Gracie's cheeks flushed. "Why would Joey Freeman care?"

"Come on, Gracie, you know Joey has liked you for years. He used to follow you home from school."

"That was when we were kids. I am grown up now. I need a man."

"What of Captain Jones? Does he know anything of this?"

Gracie blushed even more. "He hasn't said anything but he has been giving me the look. He comes to eat a lot at our fire too."

"He comes to eat at our fire, too, but nobody has

decided he wants to marry Becky." Eva teased her. Apart from Becky.

"Don't tease me, Eva. It's mean. You don't understand what it's like to love someone."

Eva wanted to correct her but couldn't.

CHAPTER 22

*E*va took some water back to her ma.

"It's very sandy, Ma."

"Captain Jones suggested putting corn meal into it before we sieve it. Seems it will remove most of the sand."

"Ma, can the girls do it? I want to check on Milly, she's been ill and looked very pale earlier."

"Of course, Eva, just don't be late for supper."

Eva found her sitting beside the wagon with no sign of a fire going.

"I have had enough, Eva, I want to go home."

"Milly, stop distressing yourself so much. It isn't good for you. Why don't you lie down for a while? The sickness is making you feel weak."

"I am so sick every morning and now my...well, I feel very sore." Milly's face flushed red as her eyes fell on her chest. "I think I might be having a baby."

"Congratulations." Eva hugged her friend but she

couldn't help think this was the last place she would want to be pregnant. The trek was hard enough without having to cope with being pregnant too. "Have you told Stan?"

"Not yet. I know he will be thrilled but it's alright for him. He isn't sick every minute of the day." Milly held a hand to her mouth. "I'm sorry, Eva, I shouldn't have said that. I just... I want to go home to my mother."

Eva held Milly while she cried. It took a while for the tears to stop. "Milly, you are exhausted. You need to sleep. I will bring over dinner for you and Stan. You need to speak to him. Tell him your news, your fears, everything. He loves you, it will be fine."

Eva walked back to her wagon, thankful they were staying at the fort for a few days. If Milly was determined to go back to Boston, then maybe they would meet other travelers here. That's assuming Stan agreed to go back.

"What has you upset, Eva?" Her ma asked gently as her eyes ran over her body.

"Ma, Milly thinks she is having a baby. She is real scared and she wants to go home. She's been crying for ages."

"Ah, the poor girl. If she is, her body is all over the place. I remember finding out I was carrying you, I couldn't stop crying for two weeks. Your pa threatened to drown me in the river."

"Did he really?"

"No, love. He was joking as he said I was in danger of drowning both of us with all my tears. I was so happy too. I had no idea why I was crying. Women go through all sorts of moods when they are carrying a young'un. You take over preparing dinner and I will go have a chat with your friend." Ma took off the apron she insisted on wearing, even though they were in the middle of the wilds. She gave it to Eva. Then she packed up a small basket with dinner and some biscuits with a small loaf of bread.

"Remind me to try the fort for some ginger tomorrow, Eva. Ginger cookies will help with the nausea."

Ma was gone for ages. Eva dished up dinner to her pa, brother and sisters as they were complaining of being hungry. She kept her own for later so Ma wouldn't have to eat alone.

She came back soon after the dishes had been done. She took Eva to one side.

"Milly feels a bit better now. I explained what it's like being pregnant. Poor girl, her ma never told her anything."

"Is she still intent on going back to Boston?" Eva hoped Milly wasn't. She loved talking to her and it made the time pass quicker. However, maybe she was being selfish. Milly might be better off in Boston.

"She's talking about it but I don't know if Stan will turn back. Anyway, that's for them to sort out."

"Being married is difficult, isn't it Ma?"

Ma laughed. "That it is, Eva, but it's wonderful too. So long as you pick the right man, of course. Now where is my dinner? I am hungry enough to eat an ox."

Eva gave her ma an impulsive hug. She hadn't heard the woman complain once on the trail, yet she must have found it difficult at times too. She was lucky to have a mother like her.

* * *

"THIS IS FORT KEARNEY?" Becky looked at the vision in front of her, unable to hide her disappointment. "There isn't even a wall around it?"

"Not what you were expecting, is it?" Eva murmured. She found it quite fascinating. There were soldiers and Indians walking around with people from other wagon trains. All sorts of people coming and going. It reminded her of market day in Virgil.

"Captain Jones said we were stopping for a couple of days so we can catch up on everything. Our laundry, chores and, of course, shopping," Ma said.

"Not too much shopping. The prices charged at these places make Harold look generous," Pa said grumpily.

"Aw, Pa, we won't buy much, but I really want a pair of moccasins. They look so pretty." Becky gave her father the look that always won him around.

"Don't spend too much, lass. We still have a long way to go."

"Thanks, Pa, you're the best." Becky gave her pa a big hug before grabbing Johanna's arm and almost running up to the vendors.

"Della, you need to have a word with that young lady. She is past the age of behaving like a child. She'll never make a good match if she runs everywhere."

"I did a lot of running and I don't think I fared too badly," Ma answered.

Eva moved away embarrassed to see her parents sharing affectionate glances. While she was pleased their arguments seemed to be a thing of the past, they were still her parents.

CHAPTER 23

*E*va went looking for the post office. She wanted to send her letters to Granny, but she was hoping there might be some for her to collect too. She didn't see the officer until she walked right into him.

"I am so sorry. I wasn't looking where I was going," she stammered as she stared up into a very attractive man's face.

He took off his hat and bowed to her. "No problem, ma'am. Not every day a pretty lady walks into me. Can I escort you to wherever you were going?"

"I was just looking to collect some posts." Eva was flustered. She wasn't used to older men taking notice of her, never mind acting in such a charming manner.

"Allow me." The officer offered his arm and she was just about to take it when she heard a shout.

"Take your hands off my fiancée."

Eva felt her face heat up as she turned to find Harold

looking threateningly at the officer who immediately apologized.

"I am very sorry. I was only offering to help your young lady in her time of need."

"I am not his young lady and I appreciate your help," Eva said, intent on taking the soldier's arm.

The officer looked at Eva in confusion. Then he turned to stare Harold down. "Is this man making you uncomfortable?" the soldier asked Eva while still looking at Harold.

"Not really. He's just an annoying boy from school. Now where is the post?" Eva smiled and fluttered her eyelashes as she had seen Becky do. She wasn't interested in the officer but she was not about to let Harold get away with shouting at her as if he owned her. The officer raised his eyebrows but gave her his arm. "This way, ma'am."

Unfortunately, there wasn't any post waiting. Eva couldn't hide her disappointment.

"I take it you were expecting something special. Another fiancé perhaps?"

Eva laughed at his joke. "I thought my granny would have written by now. We left her behind in Virgil."

"A granny I can live with but more than one fiancé a day is enough."

Eva smiled.

"My name is Wilson, Graham Wilson. There is a dance tomorrow evening. Would you be my guest?"

"Eva Thompson. I would be delighted, Mr. Wilson, but I am already going to the dance with someone else."

"The fiancé we met earlier?"

"No. I wasn't lying about him. This is someone else."
The conversation was becoming very uncomfortable.
Relieved, she spotted Becky and Johanna making their way
toward her. "My sisters, Mr. Wilson, Rebecca and
Johanna.

"It's Captain Wilson and the pleasure is all mine. Your
father must be a worried man."

"Why? Has there been some sort of trouble?" Johanna
asked, her face a mask of worry.

"Not at all, my dear, but if I had three such beautiful
daughters, I would keep my shotgun near and make sure it
was loaded."

"You frightened us, Captain Wilson. I think you may
have stayed out here in the wilds for too long." Although
Becky reprimanded him, her tone showed she was teasing.
He took her hand, kissed it, and quickly asked if she would
be free to accompany him to the ball.

"I will but you have to ask my pa. He is rather protective as you so rightly guessed," Becky said, smiling
coquettishly.

"I gather I just walked into that one. If you point me in
the direction of your father, I will make sure he knows my
intentions are fully honorable."

"Not too honorable I hope," Becky said after he walked
away.

"Shush, he will hear you. Rebecca Thompson, sometimes I wonder how you ever became my twin."

Eva smiled at the banter between her sisters. She
couldn't wait until tomorrow night. She didn't care what

her pa thought. She was going to dance, at least once, with David. That much was certain.

* * *

EARLY THE NEXT EVENING, the girls arrived at the dance. The soldiers had cleared a large area. The women of the train had each made favorite dishes and the tantalizing aromas coming from the trestle tables were making more than one man's stomach groan with appreciation.

"Good evening ladies how splendid you look." Captain Wilson bowed.

"Thank you kind sir. Without the aid of an iron or curling tongs, we had to make do." Becky's flirtatious giggle made Johanna smile. Her twin was stunning tonight as was obvious by the fact every man in the room was drawn to her like bees to honey. All except one. The one she wanted the most. Captain Jones remained chatting with some of the older officers. He seemed oblivious to the fact Becky was in the room.

"Would you like to dance Miss?"

Johanna looked up at the solider who had asked her to dance. He was so young, he still had pimples on his face. She smiled as she took his hand. The musicians were playing some sort of Irish jig. She didn't know the steps. It didn't matter as judging by the number of times her partner stepped on her toes, neither did he. She tried not to wince as he whirled her around the room.

Johanna spotted Becky dancing with Captain Wilson.

She was smiling and chatting with him but her eyes were focused on someone else. Captain Jones.   Trouble was brewing in that quarter. The more the man ignored Becky, the more she would want him.

Johanna looked around for Eva. She was dancing with Harold and looked so fed up, Johanna wished she was able to interrupt. She disliked Harold intensely. She always had. Years ago, she was walking home from school and had fallen behind Eva and Becky. She came across Harold on the bridge, trying to drown some kittens. She had ran at him and catching him by surprise was able to rescue the kittens.

Harold had been furious but thankfully he couldn't do anything to her as there were other boys around who would have protected her. David Clarke was one of them. She loved David as much as she hated Harold. It frustrated her no end, how her Pa dismissed David just because of his background. It was no more David's fault for having the town drunk as a father as it was for her being born a twin.

She spotted David watching Eva, the look of love on his face making her heart soar. Maybe she could do something to help them. She excused herself from her partner and moved over to where Eva and Harold were dancing.

"Excuse me for interrupting but the store's manager was looking for you Harold. He said something about paying you for some goods you had?" Johanna purposely looked at him blankly. "I am sorry but I wasn't really paying attention to what he said."

"Typical. Your head is always in the clouds. Come on

Eva, " Harold snapped. "I have to find out what he wanted."

"Please leave Eva here with me. I don't like being alone with a whole company of strangers." Johanna tried to flirt but given it was Harold, she failed miserably. She must have looked tortured as he agreed to go on his own.

"Thanks Jo. I was starting to wonder what I had to do to get rid of him." Eva gave her a hug.

"Pa went out, I heard him tell Ma he was going to check on the livestock but I think he has sneaked off to play cards with some of the soldiers. You and David can dance now or go for a walk if you prefer."

She was rewarded with another rib crushing hug.

"You are the best sister in the world, you know that."

She didn't get a chance to reply as Eva was gone. Hugging herself, she slipped past a group of soldiers and headed for a drink. Unfortunately, the solider who had squashed her toes found her and insisted she dance the next square dance with him. So much for one good turn deserves another. Her feet would never recover from their visit to Fort Kearney at this rate.

CHAPTER 24

*J*ohanna caught the eye of one of the men from the train. He was staring at her but it didn't give her the creeps. She had seen him around the wagons a few times but they had never spoken. He had looked at her before, his gaze making her feel beautiful. Not many people noticed her when Becky was around. She had stopped being upset years ago by the continuous comparisons between her and her livelier, more impulsive, more beautiful twin.

Could she ask him to save her? She didn't think her toes would cope with much more onslaught from the solider she was dancing with. He didn't seem to want to let her go. She had suggested once or twice they stop to get a drink but he didn't seem to hear her. She looked up again hoping to see the stranger from the wagon train but he was gone. Disappointment flooded her.

The musicians finally took a break. Her escort wanted

her to stay with him to eat but she made her excuses saying she had to find her sisters. She saw Eva and David disappear out the door. She quickly checked her Pa hadn't seen anything but he was engrossed in a conversation with some of the other older men. She looked for Becky. To her surprise, her sister was sitting alone, by the look on her face she was sulking.

"Why are you all alone?" Johanna sat beside her. "Where's Captain Wilson?"

"I've no idea. Captain Jones has been dancing with Gracie. I mean seriously. She is younger than I am and far less attractive."

"Becky! That's not fair. She may not have your more obvious beauty but Gracie is a sweet girl. I thought she was in love with Joey Freeman."

"She was back in Virgil but now she has set her sights on our Captain. Joey is fuming. He had to leave. I thought he was going to hit the Captain."

Johanna spotted Captain Jones talking to some of the women from the train. When the music started again, he asked one of the married ones to dance. Seemed to her, he was dancing with everyone not singling anyone out.

"Come on Becky, let's dance."

"Together? I am not that desperate," Becky huffed.

"Lots of the ladies are dancing. It's fun and my feet will be a lot safer with you than with some of the soldiers. Your face will curdle the cream. The worst thing you can do is let Captain Jones see you are upset. You should play hard to get remember?"

"What would you know about it Johanna? You never had a beau."

Johanna clenched her nails into the palms of her hands in a bid not to retaliate. But she didn't get a chance to as she sensed someone standing behind her.

"Good evening Miss. I wondered if you would care to dance?" He asked, smiling but his eyes were full of caution. "I am not a brilliant dancer but your feet should be safe."

Johanna's cheeks flamed. How much of their conversation had he heard? Please not the bit about her never having a beau.

She forced herself to smile and accept graciously. As soon as he touched her, tingles fled through her skin. She looked up to catch the look of surprise on his face. He had felt something too. This time her smile wasn't forced.

They danced for the rest of the evening. Dance after dance, from the square dances right through to the funny party games. She couldn't remember ever having so much fun. He didn't say much but it didn't matter. Just being with him was enough for now.

"May I walk you back to your wagon?" He asked as the musicians finished for the night.

"I don't think my pa would agree. He is very protective."

"I can understand why. I have no idea why your friend would lie about you not having beaus. I can imagine you left a trail of broken hearts on your travels here."

"My friend? Oh you mean my sister. She is always

teasing. But you are wrong. I don't make it a habit of breaking anyone's heart."

"I certainly hope not as my heart remains at your tender mercies. Good evening."

She watched as he walked away. He didn't turn back. She waited for her ma and pa to walk back to the wagon. Only then did she realize she didn't even know his name.

CHAPTER 25

"*R*ebecca Thompson, you cannot be serious. You are not staying behind at the fort."

Eva stared at her sister as their pa yelled. She had seen him annoyed before but never this bad.

"Pa, I want to stay. Graham Wilson has a wonderful career ahead of him in the army. We will be very happy together."

"You don't know the man, you only met him a couple of days ago." Pa turned to his wife. "Can you speak some sense to your daughter. I have to go for a walk."

"I love the way you become my daughter as soon as you cross your father. Seriously, Becky, what has come over you now? You don't know this man." Ma wrung her hands, something she always did when really worried.

"He's handsome and charming and a wonderful dancer. I know we will be very happy together," Becky repeated.

"I am sure he is all those things. He is also an army captain, a dangerous job at times. He will have to travel long distances leaving you for months on end alone at the fort. I don't think it will look all that glamorous then. Honestly, sometimes I wonder if I dropped you on your head when you were a baby. You are so impulsive."

Eva watched her sister closely as there was something not quite right. She wasn't pining after Captain Wilson. She hadn't even seemed that interested in him at the dance. She had been looking at Captain Jones even while dancing with Wilson.

That was it. She was using Captain Wilson as a ruse to make her real love Captain Jones look better in their parents' eyes. It was typical of her sister's mad capped ideas and she hoped it wouldn't backfire in Becky's face. Her father was hardly going to listen to declarations of love for their own captain when she had threatened to stay at the fort and marry a man she had just met.

"I think Becky is teasing you, Ma. She has a funny sense of humor." Eva decided it was time to intervene.

Becky opened her mouth but Eva sent her a warning glance. She had gone too far this time.

"Sorry, Ma, I didn't mean to upset you and Pa. I was joking. I thought it would be funny."

"Honestly, Rebeca Thompson, as if your pa and I didn't have enough to worry about."

"Ma, I am sure Becky is very sorry. She knows if she was considering marriage she should be looking for a man who is going to settle down and raise a family," Eva said trying to calm the situation.

"Listen to your sister, she is talking sense," Ma remarked.

"Someone who has proved themselves to be loyal and brave and who would do anything to protect his family. That's the type of man Pa would welcome, isn't it, Ma?"

Ma looked closely at Eva. "Are we still talking about Becky?"

Eva met her ma's gaze. She held it for several seconds before responding. "Of course, Ma, who else?"

Her ma walked off in a huff. Becky went to follow her but Eva stopped her. "You should let both of them cool down. It was rather immature to pretend you were going to stay here and marry Captain Wilson."

"How did you know what I was doing?"

"It was written all over your face at the dance. You only have eyes for one man, Becky Thompson, but you aren't going to get him by pretending to like other men."

"Ma said it's good to keep men on their toes." Becky's tone was sullen.

"She didn't say flirt with everything in trousers though. At best, Captain Jones will think you a child, at worst, something horrible like a flirt. Neither, *darling sister*, is going to capture his heart."

Eva knew she'd annoyed Becky but that wasn't the reason for what she had said. Her sister had to grow up sometime and it might as well be now. The trip was only going to get more difficult, and nobody had time for Becky's impulsiveness or her sense of humor. Not now.

* * *

THE REST HAD DONE everyone good. They started off again at a brisk pace, following the North Platte River. Captain Jones led them across the river. The crossing wasn't difficult but the waiting around was tedious. It took almost two days for everyone to cross. At times the cattle looked like they were sinking into the mud but thankfully none of them were lost.

There was no wood around so the only fuel was buffalo chips. The weather grew exceedingly hot. It was pure torture to travel inside the canvas wagon so Eva and her sisters walked. The heat was so bad even Stephen stopped smiling. It didn't help that the water of the Platte was warm and muddy making it almost impossible to drink. David and some of the other men went scouting for streams of good drinking water.

"They call this place Skunk Creek, Eva." Stephen's smile was back as he teased her. She certainly hoped they didn't come across any of those hateful creatures. They smelled bad enough without that. Everywhere they looked, they saw hundreds of wagons. It was almost as if the entire USA had decided to move west. The resulting trails were very sandy in places making travel more uncomfortable.

"At least with every mile we cover, we are getting

closer to Oregon," Johanna said as she wiped yet more dust from her face and neck. Eva could have strangled her sister. Judging by the look Becky sent her, she wasn't the only one.

"Look, Eva, David's coming. He looks happy."

Eva shielded her eyes from the sun. Stephen was right. David was smiling.

"We found a lovely stream just a little bit from here. You can go swimming and everything."

"Is the water nice?" Becky asked.

"Try it for yourself." David handed her his canteen. "Just leave some for your sisters and brother."

The water was cold and tasted better than anything she had to drink for some time. The oxen picked up the scent of water, too, as they moved quicker in the direction David had pointed.

"Some of the stream is quite deep but in parts it is only six inches. You can bathe in peace."

Stephen ran into the stream and started splashing them. Eva looked at her sisters and suddenly they all ran in and dunked their little brother. None of them cared that it was not appropriate for three young ladies to be standing soaked to the skin. The water was bliss, especially after the long hot days. Their ma and pa laughed at their antics in the water. Eva caught a look in her ma's eyes that suggested the older woman was tempted to join them. But she didn't.

After some time enjoying themselves, they got back to their chores. The girls washed out the laundry while

Stephen helped their pa fill the water barrels on the wagon.

The grass was excellent, too, so both humans and livestock enjoyed their stay at the creek.

CHAPTER 26

The soldiers at the fort had warned them there was some trouble with the Indians. Although most of the tribes were peaceful, some younger braves were getting fed up with the number of white people trailing across what they saw as their land. The numbers of buffalo being killed—in their view senselessly—was also an issue. The over landers only ate certain parts of the buffalo leaving the rest for wolves and other wild animals. The Indians used every piece of its carcass.

David watched as the Indian braves moved closer to the train. He saw Captain Jones riding back. He had been scouting up ahead. David looked around at the other men who were standing watching, but nobody had taken out their guns. Hopefully, the Indians were only interested in trading.

The Indians came in slowly. David had read that was a good sign. If it had been a war party, they would have raced in and taken them by surprise. Still, he wasn't letting his guard down yet. The wagons had slowed but not formed a circle.

Captain Jones greeted the leader of the Indians, so David rode slowly to Captain Jones' side as a couple of braves escorted their leader. He didn't want to show a sign of force, but he didn't want the Indians believing Captain Jones was alone either. David didn't understand what they were saying but Captain Jones did.

"Clarke, tell the women the Indian squaws want to trade. Tell them to hide anything that glitters unless they want to part with it. Diamond rings catch the light and the squaws love them. They don't know their value. Tell the women to barter hard, it's part of the experience. The squaws love to haggle."

David nodded at Jones and the Indian chief before riding slowly back to camp. Captain Jones had told him how to behave in front of Indians—it wasn't a lesson he was about to forget. He went from wagon to wagon telling the women what Captain Jones said. He also told a few of the men to remember the Indians didn't have the same sense of humor as the whites so to tread carefully.

The women were glad of the chance to break the monotony of the trip and soon the grasses around the wagons were full of women, white and Indian, laughing and gesturing as they swapped moccasins and beads for brushes, mirrors or other feminine fancies. David smiled as he saw Eva in the middle of the crowd, a smile of delight on her face. He was watching her so closely he didn't notice a smaller crowd of braves had surrounded a wagon. A girl's scream pierced the air causing fear and consternation to break out.

David rode toward the scream trying to pace himself the entire time. He didn't want to make a bad situation worse. Mr. Bradley was being held by the arms by two Indians while his daughter, Gracie, stood still as a statue. By the look on her face, David guessed she was in shock. What woman wouldn't be as she stood with three Indian braves pulling at her hair?

Captain Jones and the Indian chief rode up. The chief barked something at the braves. They took a step back but didn't release their hold on Gracie.

"Indian braves all want red-haired woman as squaw. They didn't mean make offense. How many horses you take for woman?"

David wasn't sure which was more shocking: the Indian chief speaking broken English, or the fact that they wanted to trade horses for a white woman. Gracie's face lost more color and she looked as if she would pass out any second. He admired her courage. Most girls would be lying in a dead faint by now.

"Tell them they can have her for ten horses. Whoever brings the best horses can have her."

"Shut up, Bradley." Captain Jones growled but it was too late.

The chief had understood Bradley's price and relayed it to his braves. The three braves ran and vaulted onto some horses and rode off before anyone could do anything.

"Chief, Bradley did not understand. He doesn't want to trade his daughter," Captain Jones tried to reason with the Indian leader.

"But he name price. Trade must proceed unless horses are not to his satisfaction."

Eva had moved to David's side by this stage. "What's going on? Poor Gracie looks like she saw a ghost," Eva whispered to David.

"Her father just told the Indians he would trade her for ten horses."

"What? But he was joking." Eva looked around. "They didn't take him seriously, did they?"

"Afraid so. Captain Jones is trying to sort it out. But you best tell the others to be on their guard. Tell the women to stay close to camp and not to let the children wander far."

"I will but first I am going to bring Gracie to Ma. No wonder she looks so scared. She isn't even crying," Eva said softly.

"She's in shock. Needs a hot drink."

David watched as Eva moved quickly but quietly to Gracie's side. Taking her hand, she pulled her away from the group. Eva was a brave girl. Bit too brave if David was being honest. He didn't want any of the Indian braves getting any ideas about taking Eva for a squaw.

* * *

EVA HELD Gracie's hand tightly as she led the poor girl toward Ma. Telling Ma the story quickly, she left Gracie with her and went to find some hot coffee. Coming back, she found Ma gently reassuring Gracie, who was sitting wrapped in a blanket, a vacant look on her face.

"What was Mr. Bradley thinking? Captain Jones told us the Indians didn't find our sense of humor funny."

"I know, Eva, but I guess nobody thought they would think a man would give up his daughter for ten horses," Ma said without taking her gaze from Gracie.

"I'd sell my sisters for one horse. I'd love my own pony," Stephen added but a swift slap across the back of his legs had him running off toward the children.

"Cheeky little beggar," Ma said but her eyes told Eva she was trying not to laugh.

"What do you think will happen, Ma?"

"I don't know, darling. I have faith in Captain Jones. He'll see us out of this mess. You will see."

Eva hoped her mother was right. She couldn't imagine leaving her family to live with Indians. Gracie stayed with the Thompsons all night. Ma insisted it wouldn't be right to send her back to Mr. Bradley who, by all accounts, was distraught at what he'd done.

CHAPTER 27

*E*va took a chance to sneak off to speak to David. She figured her ma was caught up with Gracie and her pa was over talking to the other men. David was on guard duty at the rear of the wagon. She took her time moving as quietly as possible to where he was standing.

"Eva, I could have shot you."

"Quiet or you will bring everyone over to us. I had to talk to you." Eva gave him a quick hug ignoring the fact he didn't return her embrace. He was angry but this was too important. "What's going to happen tomorrow?"

"You mean when the Indians find out the trade won't happen?" David asked tonelessly.

"Yes. Do you think they will attack the caravan?"

David stayed quiet a couple of seconds too long. Eva's heart started thumping harder.

"Captain Jones has a lot of experience with Indians. He will make them understand."

"You don't really believe that, do you?" Eva said hoping he would contradict her.

"It doesn't matter what I think. We have to believe in Captain Jones. The alternative doesn't bear thinking about." David took a deep breath. "Did you hear about Joey?"

"Freeman? No."

"Captain Jones had to order his pa to keep him under guard. You know how he feels about Gracie. He was all set to ride after the Indians and kill them before they put a hand on her again."

"Poor Joey." Eva shivered. "David, hold me, please. I'm scared."

David drew her into his arms, kissing her gently on the top of her head. "Eva, nothing will happen to you. You know how to shoot. Remember what I told you before."

"Always leave one bullet just in case."

"Yes, darling, but we won't be shooting tomorrow. Now you best get back or you will be missed and then there will be trouble." He kissed her lightly on the lips before giving her a quick hug and pushing her in the direction of the camp. "Go on now."

Eva glanced once over her shoulder to see him smiling at her before making her way back to the wagon. Pa wasn't back but her ma was waiting for her at the fire.

"Where have you been, or do I need to ask?" Ma said.

Eva debated telling her a lie but decided honesty was best. "I had to go see David. I wanted to make sure he was alright. We could all be..." Eva's voice trembled. Her ma moved quickly to her side and drew her into a hug surprising both of them.

"Don't fret, child. Captain Jones will sort everything out, and we will soon be on our way."

"But, Ma..."

"We have to trust, Eva, love. No sense in anticipating bad things." Ma moved slightly but didn't release her hold on Eva. "So David Clarke still holds your heart?"

Eva stared at her ma.

Ma laughed. "I was young and in love once too, you know. You don't have to say anything. It's written all over your face. And his, I should add. Your granny thinks a lot of him."

Eva nodded too stunned to ask her ma how she knew that.

"No point talking about how Granny feels about him. Pa is set on a match with Harold." Eva couldn't control the shiver of revulsion coursing through her body.

"Your pa only wants what is best for you, Eva."

"David is best for me. He loves me. I don't know why Harold is even interested in me. I don't have any money and I am not the best-looking girl on the caravan. He could do much better," Eva burst out, her frustration at the situation piling over.

"Eva Thompson, don't you let me hear you talk about yourself like that. Any man would be lucky to have you as a wife." Ma looked annoyed. Eva kicked herself for saying anything. She didn't want to ruin the intimacy. Her ma rarely spoke to her like an adult.

"Sorry, Ma."

"I know we have taught you pride is a sin but that doesn't mean you need to put yourself down either. Far too many folk are willing to do that for you." Ma smiled. "I think David may disagree with your view of yourself. From where I am sitting, he seems to think you would make a fine partner."

Eva blushed, glad the darkness was hiding most of the heat in her face.

"Ma, do you think...will Pa ever change his mind about David?"

Her ma stared into the flames taking her time to answer. "Your pa doesn't often admit when he is wrong about someone. But this whole experience has shown us different things. Spending so much time in our neighbors' company has been enlightening. Delightfully so in some cases but there are those I cannot wait to leave behind."

Eva didn't speak. She hoped her ma had David in the former category.

"We are all finding out a lot of things not only about our vast country but about ourselves and each other. Your pa will make the right decision in the end. He is motivated by your happiness regardless of what it appears like now."

"Why can't he see marrying Harold would make me dreadfully unhappy?" Eva's voice wavered as she fought tears of frustration.

"Your pa grew up hungry, Eva. Not just hungry like we are when the ground is muddy and we can't get a good fire going. I mean hungry all the time, day and night.

When your grandpa died, the family became very poor. They didn't have anything and that feeling has stuck with your pa. He's worked very hard to provide his family with a good home. He never wants any of his children to suffer like he did."

"David is a hard worker too."

"Yes, he is but David's pa casts a legacy your pa is finding difficult to ignore. Also, you and your pa are very alike. You are both stubborn. The more you push back against your pa over his choices the more resistant he will become."

"You mean, if I agreed to marry Harold tomorrow, he would welcome David with open arms."

"Don't be bitter, Eva, it doesn't suit you. Of course, that won't happen. But with patience, you may find all of us understand each other better by the end of this trip. I know you think you love David, but that is not enough for a good marriage. You have to like him too. You have to be able to put up with his bad points, everyone has them, as well as his good ones. Only when you can do that, should you consider marriage to anyone."

Eva didn't reply. She knew her ma was right. Patience. It was so hard when all she wanted was to spend every minute of every day with David.

"I'll try, Ma."

"Good girl."

"Where's Gracie?" she asked in an attempt to change the subject.

"Poor girl is still shocked. I told her, Becky and

Johanna to share the feather bed in the wagon. You will have to squash in there too," Ma said, a worried expression on her face. "Poor Gracie thinks the braves will sneak in tonight and whisk her away."

"David told me Joey Freeman had to be put under guard. He's desperate to protect Gracie."

"Another fine young man. Joey Freeman will make Gracie a good husband. A much more suitable match than Captain Jones."

Ma's words surprised Eva. She didn't know how her ma knew about Gracie's infatuation with Captain Jones. But her ma hadn't finished.

"Gracie and your sister won't be the first, or the last, young girls to have their head turned by an older man."

Eva didn't want to discuss Becky's infatuation with Captain Jones with her ma. Instead, she desperately tried to change the subject.

"Poor Gracie. I bet she could shake her pa," Eva said.

"Don't judge Mr. Bradley. He's been doing the best he can since poor Mrs. Bradley succumbed to the fever. I think losing his wife and two young'uns has affected his mind. The poor man. We didn't do enough to help reduce his burden."

Typical of her ma to think of someone else. She wished she could be more like her mother. Instead, she had a fiery temper and was too quick to voice her opinion.

"Now why don't you go into the wagon and get some sleep? Your pa and I will sleep in the tent tonight. Not that I think the menfolk will be doing much sleeping."

"Good night, Ma. Thank you." She gave her ma a quick kiss on the cheek before climbing into the wagon. She was surprised to find both Gracie and Becky asleep. Johanna was praying and Stephen was looking out trying to spot Indians.

"You best try and sleep. If Pa catches us awake, he will have something to say about it."

"Aw, do I have to?"

"Go to sleep, Stephen," Eva and Johanna said at the same time causing laughter. It was rather squashed in the wagon but Eva felt safer. She prayed David was wrong and tomorrow would pass off peacefully.

CHAPTER 28

orning came quickly. There was an uneasy
atmosphere around the camp as they
prepared to leave. Captain Jones had spread word they
were to behave as if it was a normal day. They had
pancakes and bacon for breakfast and for once everyone
was ready before they started out at 4 am. Captain Jones
decided not to sound the gunshots like they did every
morning. "No point in inviting trouble," he said as he rode
past.

Eva hoped David was driving the wagon rather than
out on guard duty. She knew she was being selfish but she
wanted him as safe as possible. They made good progress
that morning but they couldn't outrun the Indians. It
wasn't long before Captain Jones signaled for the wagon
train to stop. They waited, as the Indian braves rode up
alongside the captain, herding lots of horses.

"Looks like they took old man Bradley seriously. There

are about forty horses there." Stephen jumped up and down trying to see over the adult's heads.

"Go back to the wagon and settle down. We don't need any more mistakes." Pa spoke sharply causing Stephen to obey immediately. Ma held Gracie's arm on one side, Joey Freeman held the other.

Gracie had said she would accept what her father had done rather than risk the lives of the people on the train. Thankfully, Captain Jones told her he appreciated her offer but wasn't about to stand by and leave a white woman behind. He had surprised them all by letting Joey stand with Gracie. Joey had a gun and had vowed to shoot Gracie before letting anyone ride off with her. Captain Jones had taken his gun away but allowed Joey to hold Gracie's hand.

Eva watched as the captain and the chief exchanged words. She couldn't understand what they were saying but it was obviously becoming heated. David arrived to join them, his arms nearly buckling under the weight of skins and hides. Eva realized that's what her pa and the other men had been up to. They had collected items from every wagon in order to trade with the Indian braves. Hopefully, they would be so pleased with the bounty they would receive they would forget about Gracie. Initially, it didn't look as if the tactic would work.

Ma broke loose from Gracie's grasp and took something out of the back of the wagon. Head held high, she approached the men and laid the basket at the Indian chief's feet. She bowed and walked backward to where

Eva was standing, all the while not once looking any Indian man in the face. Other women followed Ma's example. The baskets were full of pies and cookies. The chief tasted a few things—Eva shuddered to see his eating habits—but it was obvious he enjoyed the gifts. He shared some with the other braves who ate hungrily.

"Your ma is a miracle worker. It was her idea to get the other women to bake things for the chief. She read somewhere the Indians have a sweet tooth."

Eva smiled up at David who was whispering to her out of the side of his mouth. "Like any man—the way to their heart is through their stomach," she whispered back making him smile.

Eva felt Gracie shivering beside her. It must feel like forever for the young girl as the Indians and Captain Jones negotiated. Finally, Captain Jones shook the chief's hand. The chief barked something at his men and they all fell back taking the horses with them. Gracie almost fell into Joey's arms. Eva smiled thinking this was a turning point in her friend's relationship. There would be no more talk of Gracie and Captain Jones.

"Do you think they would leave just one pony for me?" Stephen asked as he peeked his head out from behind the canvas cover.

"Get away from there before your pa spots you," Ma hissed as they made their way back to the wagon. The crowd dispersed quietly following Captain Jones' instructions to move out quickly and quietly.

The wagon train pulled out as instructed. The danger

seemed to have passed. Joey had to go back on guard duty so Gracie stayed with the Thompsons. Ma felt she needed some female company. Eva reckoned now that the Indians had gone, Gracie might have something to say to her pa. Ma was trying to keep the peace between them.

* * *

David pulled up by their wagon later that evening. They were traveling later than usual trying to put as many miles between the Indians and the train.

"Eva, keep Gracie inside the wagon. It's best she doesn't show her face for a day or so."

"Why?"

"Seems one of the braves hasn't taken the chief's decision very well. He is following behind."

Eva looked beyond David's head as if the brave would materialize any minute.

"I think the poor fellow reckons he is in love. He keeps asking for his Red lady. Hopefully, he will get fed up but it's best to be careful."

"David Clarke, is that you visiting again?" Ma's voice alerted them to her presence.

"Yes, Mrs. Thompson. Just telling Eva, I mean Miss Thompson, one of the braves who wanted to take Miss Bradley was tracking us."

"We will keep Gracie inside the wagon. Thank you for the warning. You are welcome to join us for supper, if you like, when Captain Jones tells us we can stop."

"Thank you, Mrs. Thompson. I would be honored."

Eva could have jumped up and down with happiness but she said nothing. She couldn't even look at David as he rode away. She knew her ma was watching her closely.

Captain Jones gave them permission to stop later that evening. It was too dangerous to try to travel in the dark. Eva hoped her ma remembered she had invited David to eat with them. She brushed and braided her hair before securing it with a ribbon he had bought her. It was silly to be so excited about seeing him. It had only been a few hours.

* * *

DAVID TOOK a deep breath telling himself it was a chance to impress Mr. Thompson. He had never eaten with the family before. Mrs. Long had given him some cookies she had made earlier that day. She knew of his love for Eva. He hadn't said anything, so she must have guessed from different things he said or did.

"Thank you very much for inviting me this evening, Mrs. Thompson. Mr. Thompson, Mrs. Long thought you might appreciate these after your meal."

He handed Eva's father the cookies after shaking his hand. Mr. Thompson wasn't rude but he was hardly welcoming either.

David risked a quick glance at Eva. She looked so pretty and she was wearing his ribbon. He immediately felt better.

"So what's your plan for Oregon then, young lad?"

"I want to claim some land and start my own farm." David risked a quick glance at Eva. "I plan on getting married and raising my own family."

"Not easy being a farmer." Mr. Thompson sucked on his pipe making his words difficult to follow.

"No, sir, but I am a hard worker. I plan on being successful. I want my wife and children to have plenty."

"And what of the drink?"

"Pa, please stop. Ma?" Eva begged but David cleared his throat.

"It's a fair question, Eva, I mean, Miss Thompson." David felt his collar tighten around his neck at his error. "I don't drink, Mr. Thompson, and never plan on starting. I have seen firsthand how it destroys families."

He met Mr. Thompsons gaze not willing to be the first to look away. He thought he spotted a glimmer of admiration in the older man's eyes but it was difficult to tell by firelight.

"I must say you seem to be doing very well with the Long family. Captain Jones is often singing your praises, too, young man."

"Thank you, Mrs. Thompson. It is easy traveling with the Longs. They are good people. Captain Jones gives clear instructions so I have not found it difficult to obey him either," David said hoping he didn't come across as boasting. He was proud of his achievements but he knew pride wasn't a quality most valued.

CHAPTER 29

The encounter with the Indians was soon forgotten as they faced another major hurdle on their trip. Everyone was nervous. It had rained for the best part of the week and they were coming to a dangerous river crossing. Captain Jones moved through the train telling people to waterproof their wagons even those taking the ferry.

The families who had elected not to take the ferry were being rope towed across the river. They had to secure everything inside their wagons. With any luck, the wagon would stay afloat as it was towed across, but with strong water currents, they really needed all the luck they could get.

Eva snuck out again to see David. She wanted him to tell her it would all be fine.

"David, you are soaking wet." Eva pushed him away but he only cuddled her closer.

"Everyone and everything is wet. The rain hasn't stopped for a week. Although it seems to have stopped now. Some of the older folks are saying it will be dry tomorrow."

They both shivered under the tree. The good side of it raining meant there was plenty of green grass for the animals to graze on. The downside was the ground was getting muddy which increased the risk of an accident. Also, the rain had caused the river to swell, and Eva was nervous enough about crossing them.

"David, has Captain Jones said anything about the river crossing tomorrow?" When he didn't say anything, she looked into his eyes and saw the worry and concern.

"Eva, warn your pa that the river is very deep."

Eva shivered, not wanting to think about the implications. "Pa won't listen to me but I'll try. Are you driving the Long wagon?"

"No. I convinced the Longs to take the ferry. I know it is more expensive but it's safer."

Eva guessed David was helping the Longs cover the cost. He was looking everywhere but at her. "I love the way you are looking out for that family."

She caught the look of relief on his face. Surely, he didn't think she begrudged the Long family his time and attention.

"Thanks, Eva. Mr. Long, well, he is the first man in a while to treat me right from the get go. I dunno... I feel like I owe him."

"I understand, David, truly I do. I love you more for it."

David's face nearly split with the size of his grin. "Is your pa taking the ferry?"

"He said he would but Harold is trying to talk him out of it. Says it's a waste of money." Eva saw David's face darken at Harold's name.

"I hope your pa has more sense than to listen to that..."

"Ma does anyway. She's insisting on waiting for the ferry as she wants to take some time to do laundry if it's dry. At least that's her excuse. I best go and help or she will send out a search party." Eva coughed trying to steady her voice. "Be careful, David. See you on the other side."

"Eva, don't be nervous. The ferry will be quite safe."

"But everyone isn't taking the ferry, are they? Some are going to try and cross without it."

"The ferry is expensive. Not everyone can afford it. But there are enough of us men around to make sure everyone will cross safely." David sounded confident but his eyes were cloudy with worry.

"You won't put yourself in danger, will you? I couldn't bear it if I lost you."

David kissed her lightly on the lips. "I'll be careful. Now stop worrying, you are leaving frown marks on your forehead."

He kissed the so called marks away.

Eva heard her ma calling for her.

"I got to get back. She can't find us like this."

With one last kiss, Eva made her way back to the wagon.

"There you are. I need some help. Your pa and brother

had some luck. They caught a couple of trout. Can you clean them while I sort out the fire?"

"Yes, Ma." Eva didn't mind cleaning fish as it would make a welcome change from their current diet. She wondered how Milly was faring. She hadn't seen her much in the last few days. The rain made everyone stick closer to their wagons. She must check on her tomorrow before they crossed the river.

* * *

THE NEXT DAY STARTED EARLY. It was a lovely sunny day just as the older folk had predicted. The livestock and most of the teams were the first to be herded across the river. Eva and her sisters watched open mouthed as their father and some of the other men worked hard to make sure the animals crossed safely.

Ma was determined they would stay busy rather than wallow in their fear. "If we have to wait all day to find out when we cross, we might as well get some work done."

"Ma, this water is stone cold. How are we supposed to wash the clothes?"

"Like this. You get plenty of strong soap and make sure you scrub the dirt off. I won't have my standards dropping just because we aren't back at home."

"But, Ma, the lye soap makes my hands hurt. Can't Eva do it? She's better at washing than me."

"Only because she's had more practice. I have a good mind to make you do all the laundry by yourself, Becky

Thompson, only we don't have time. But if you whine one more time you will go to bed without supper tonight."

It was unusual for Ma to be so grumpy. Eva guessed Ma was worried about the river crossing. The whole atmosphere around the wagons was tense. It was their first attempt to cross such a wide river and while people had faith in Captain Jones, they were still nervous.

Eva rubbed the clothes viciously as she thought of Harold trying to persuade her pa to take risks. All to save money. How many dollars did that man need? It was embarrassing the way he flaunted his wealth among the other wagon owners. The men didn't like the way he flirted with their wives and teenage daughters either.

Eva hadn't said anything to her ma as she didn't want anyone thinking she was jealous. She wasn't. The sooner Harold got married to someone else the better. But for some reason he was still stuck on her. She had no idea why. She was rude to him whenever he called. She was no real beauty and did not have a big dowry so whatever the attraction was, she couldn't see it.

After rinsing the clothes in cold water, they hung them on the nearest bushes to dry. Her pa came back just as they finished. "It will be our turn in about an hour."

"Are you taking the ferry?"

"Yes. I know it costs but I think young Harold is being foolish. You can't always make decisions based on the dollar cost alone."

Eva saw relief fill her ma's eyes. She had been worried too.

CHAPTER 30

Waiting for their turn on the ferry proved nerve wracking. Eva wished they had the chance to go first. It was better than sitting on the river bank watching everyone else go in front of them. The ferry didn't look too strong either, yet it crossed back and forth with no problems.

"There's Harold. He's not taking the ferry. Pa thought he had talked him around. He must have changed his mind," Johanna said pointing at the river.

The girls watched as Harold's wagon was towed across. About halfway to the other side, a current caused the wagon to lurch. They stood up, sure Harold and his goods would be thrown into the river, but thankfully he got to the other side without further mishap.

Next it was the Longs turn to cross on the ferry. Eva prayed hard as David traveled with the family across the river but they too made it over safely.

"It will be our turn soon. I can't wait until we are over on the other side. I am not going to open my eyes until I feel hard ground underneath my feet again," Johanna declared.

Becky teased her for being scared. Eva could see her sister was enjoying every minute of the action. She really didn't scare easily.

It was their turn next. They made it onto the ferry smoothly. The water was flowing over the deck of the ferry making Eva feel worse. What if they sank? How would they swim in the water with their dresses? It would be impossible to swim in those currents regardless of how they were dressed. The ferry moved slowly. It seemed to move back more than forward but finally they were almost to the other side.

"That's Stan and Milly beside us. I thought they would get the ferry too," Becky said watching the other wagon. Eva followed her sisters gaze. She could see Milly sitting up front in the wagon beside her husband. Her face was whiter than the canvas of the wagon.

"Come on, Milly, you will be fine," Eva whispered. Milly wouldn't be able to hear her if she shouted and she didn't want to cause any alarm. She watched her friends wagon, all fear of their own ferry crossing gone.

It seemed to be going smoothly until they heard a loud crash. A strong wave had hit the front part of the wagon— the bit where the rope connected the wagon to the oxen pulling it on the far shore. Eva watched as Stan made a grab for the rope which was thrashing about. He almost made it but another wave hit him off course knocking him into the river. Milly's screams could be heard on both sides of the river now. Milly stood up in the wagon. People shouted at her to sit back down. The wagon was rocking from side to side in the current.

"Oh, what are they going to do?" Johanna closed her eyes.

"Eva, look someone is in the water. They are swimming towards Stan. There is someone else going to help Milly. Whoever they are, please God let them get to her in time," Becky said, scanning the river.

Eva and her sisters prayed. They couldn't do anything else. Eva watched mesmerized as she realized it was David and Captain Jones who had gone to Milly's aid.

Becky grabbed her arm. "It's Captain Jones. And David Clarke. Aren't they so brave?"

Eva couldn't say anything. She watched horrified as the current fought the two men. She prayed harder than she ever did before.

"They got Stan, he's out of the water!" Johanna shrieked joyfully. "He seems to be alive."

Eva couldn't think about Stan. She watched as David and Captain Jones both got battered again and again by the current. Milly seemed to be stuck to her seat.

The Thompsons' wagon reached the shore. Her father and Stephen helped them take the wagon off. Eva couldn't do anything but stare at the river. She felt a hand on her shoulder.

"He will be fine. He is an excellent swimmer," her ma said.

"We must build a good strong fire and make some hot drinks. They will need it when they come out. The water is very cold."

Eva helped the others gather firewood for a large fire. Her ma organized the other women to make pots of coffee and something hot to eat. It was only then she remembered Stan had been pulled from the water. She went to find out how he was.

"He's out cold but so long as the bang on his head isn't too serious he should be fine. Thanks to Harold." Pa said.

"Harold?"

"Yes, Eva, Harold was the one who reached him. He dragged him out of the river. Your young man is quite a hero."

"He's not my man," Eva responded sharply earning her a look from her father but before he could say anything else a shout of joy went up from the spectators on the river bank. She rushed to the edge trying to get past the people crowded there. She was just in time to see a very wet David and Captain Jones fall ashore. Milly was also wet but unharmed. Eva wanted to go to David but she couldn't get through the throng. Anyway, Milly needed her.

She put her arm around her friend helping her toward the fire Ma had got going.

"You need to change your clothes. Ma probably has something to fit you until we get your own things dried out." Eva didn't know how much of their wagon had survived. Milly hadn't spoken a word—which scared her more than anything.

"Ma, come help us, please." She drew her ma away from the crowd. Milly's condition wasn't generally known. Her ma got some hot coffee and practically poured it into the freezing young woman. She stripped her off and redressed her in warm dry clothes, all the time telling her that her husband was alive and well. But Milly still didn't stay anything. She kept closing her eyes.

"Let her sleep in the feather bed in our wagon. Stan isn't awake yet. She's in shock, poor girl."

Ma cuddled Milly like she would her own daughter until the girl was fast asleep. Only then did she realize Eva was still with her.

"Eva, go check how David and Captain Jones are."

"But Pa..."

"Leave your pa to me. Go on, darling. I know you want to be at his side. He did you proud today."

Eva gave her ma a grateful hug before heading out to find David and Captain Jones. They were at the center of attention along with Harold, all three men being called heroes by the other travelers. It took a while but eventually she reached David's side. He spotted her and pulled away from his admirers. He was wrapped in a blanket, still shivering despite having changed out of his wet clothes.

"You are awfully brave," she whispered into his chest as he held her in his arms. "I was so scared."

"I had to do something. I couldn't leave her out there alone."

"I know that and I am proud of you but next time leave it to someone else, please?" She begged, although knowing David as well as she did, she knew he would never stop to think of himself.

"I love you, David Clarke."

"I love you, too, Eva Thompson. I think it might be time to have the conversation with your pa. After everything today, it just shows us how unpredictable life can be."

"Not today but soon. Ma will work on Pa, she'll help us."

Sighing, Eva gave herself up to his kiss. She didn't care who saw them anymore.

* * *

SOMEONE WAS WATCHING them and the look on his face would have turned Eva's blood to ice if she'd seen him. Just you wait Clarke. You won't get away with stealing my girl.

CHAPTER 31

The weather turned dry and warm but not too hot. It made walking the trail much easier. It was still hard work. The walking was tiring enough without having to do chores, too, but Eva considered herself lucky. Since the river crossing, nothing bad had happened. There had been no accidents or serious mishaps, nobody was ill and they were making good progress on their journey.

Milly and her husband, Stan, had both fully recovered. Milly hadn't lost her baby, something her ma confided later she had been sure would happen. Stan had a broken arm but it seemed to be healing nicely.

Her friend seemed happier. Milly said the knock to Stan's head had woken him up a little. He'd realized he wasn't cut out to be a farmer or perhaps more importantly Milly wasn't ready to be a farmer's wife. He'd promised Milly they would stop in the first decent sized town they came across. Milly was content with that. Milly had said to Eva that she might make it to Oregon yet, but she wasn't going to say that to Stan in case he thought her strong enough to take up farming. The girls had giggled at the idea of Milly sowing or reaping a harvest. "My hands and nails are already ruined. If Mother could see me now, I think she would swoon," Milly said holding up her chapped hands.

Eva was glad her friend was so happy, but she was worried about her own situation. Harold's rescue of Stan seemed to have redeemed him in Pa's eyes. Pa wasn't a mean man. He had commented on David's bravery and shook his hand but it was Harold he invited to have meals with the family. Eva had tried talking to her ma but she was distracted. Becky's admiration for Captain Jones had increased, and Ma was concerned her younger daughter was going to make a fool of herself.

Eva snuck out at night to see David but it wasn't enough. He was losing patience too. He wanted to speak to her pa. They had a huge row with David accusing Eva of liking the way Harold was following her around like a lovesick puppy.

* * *

"Captain Jones is worried about the Indian's who are trailing us."

"Stop it, Becky. You are scaring Johanna." Eva's impatience was at an all-time low.

"The Indians didn't hurt us last time, why would they do something now?" Johanna asked.

"'Cause these are a different tribe. The nice ones were left on the other side of the river. Scott said these ones are angry."

"Since when has Captain Jones become Scott?" Eva said, her anger at her younger sister spilling over. "I have a good mind to talk to Pa."

"No, you can't do that, Eva," The twins said in unison.

Before Eva could say anything else, Stephen ran over to them.

"Look, there's Courthouse Rock. My teacher told me we'd see it. Chimney Rock will be up ahead."

"Why do they call it Chimney Rock?"

"'Cause of its shape, silly. it looks like a chimney pointed up to heaven."

"You'll be heading towards heaven if you call me silly again," Becky replied to her brother's teasing.

"You will have to catch me first." Stephen scampered off leaving his sisters laughing in his wake.

"Come on girls, we have to see if we can find some wood. I don't fancy eating sea biscuits again.

"Who would have thought we'd miss gathering buffalo chips? We have changed a lot in the past few months, haven't we?"

Nobody answered Johanna's question. Eva guessed they were all thinking about how far they had come and the distance they still had left to travel.

* * *

Eva snuck out that evening for a walk with David. Now her ma knew how she felt and often covered for her.

"Don't you let me down, girl. I don't mind you walking with young Clarke but make sure that's all you do."

"Yes, Ma." She colored, hoping her ma interpreted it as embarrassment over the implication and not guilt over the fact that she liked kissing David and had no intention of stopping.

"We made it to Scotts Bluff. Captain Jones said this is just about the nicest scenery for a while."

Eva looked around her. The cedar trees dotted along the horizon did give it a pretty view but the story behind the name made her sad.

"The last couple of days without proper fuel will soon be behind us. I never want to taste another sea biscuit again."

"Tomorrow we will camp in a cottonwood grove. Plenty of water and wood for fuel. You will be able to wash my socks."

She gave him a playful nudge. "You can wash your own smelly socks. We're not married yet."

He pulled her into his arms so suddenly she shrieked. He quieted her with a kiss. "We will be soon and you best be good at washing socks," he teased as he punctuated each word with a kiss. Sighing she pulled his head down so she could capture his mouth. If only they were already married.

"You know why they call it Scotts Bluff, don't you?"

"Yes, Eva, but don't dwell on that poor man. He was brave. He knew he was going to die and sent his companions on to safety. That is true bravery."

Eva didn't respond. She never wanted to be in a situation where she had to choose a lonely death over the safety of those she loved.

"Is Captain Jones determined not to stop at Fort Laramie?"

"No, we are making good progress but he wants to be sure we get through the mountains before it snows. He will let people ride in with letters and to collect post but we won't camp there like we did at Fort Kearney."

David proved to be right. The train passed by Fort Laramie barely stopping long enough to post their letters. There was no mail for Eva, but she didn't have time to dwell on the disappointment. She was looking forward to seeing Devil's Gate. She had read about it in the guidebooks but knew seeing it in person would be even better.

"Look, Eva, those cliffs on either side are about four hundred feet. Captain Jones said so."

Eva smiled at her brother. Captain Jones was his idol. He had given up all ideas of being a farmer like his pa. Now he wanted to be a trail guide just like the captain. "Can you come see it with me? You know Ma won't let me get close if I go on my own."

Eva held his hand so he wouldn't get too excited and fall over. They looked at all the names carved into the stones.

"Eva, some of these names have been here twenty years. That's longer than you've been born. They are so old."

Eva laughed at her brother's face. She supposed to a seven-year-old, twenty was old. He must think their parents were ancient.

CHAPTER 32

*J*ohanna once again gathered the children together to walk down the cut offs. Not only was the dust bad but the Ellis family had contracted cholera. Mrs. Ellis and two of her children had died.

Captain Jones had suggested taking the children away so they wouldn't see the burial. Johanna had only known Mrs. Ellis by sight but Benjy had come with the children a few times. She couldn't believe she wouldn't see his smiling face again.

She took the children down one cut off. Julia suggested they sing a song but nobody was in the mood. Children understood more than their elders gave them credit.

"Benjy and Baby George are dead, Carrie and Sarah are still sick aren't they Jo? That's why they didn't come with us today." Almanzo's eyes were full of tears but he was battling not to cry. Her heart melted at the sight of such a young boy trying to be a grown up. They had reached the edge of a small stream. "Let's sit here for a while and pray for the Ellis family."

"Benjy will be singing up in Heaven now with Baby George and their ma. I pity Mr. Ellis. He will be so lonely now with only Sarah and Carrie for company."

Johanna hugged Julia. "Yes Mr. Ellis and the girls will need our help. They are going to feel sad for a while."

"I would hate to lose any of my family. I love them all even if my big sisters are annoying."

"Rachel and Louisa are lovely girls, Julia. They just forget what it is like to be six years old," Johanna attempted to cheer Julia up. "My older sister, Eva, can be a pain too but most of the time she is nice."

"I like Eva. She comes to sit at our fire sometimes when David is there. She sure looks funny when she stares at him. Her eyes go all gooey," Julia demonstrated a puppy dog face making Johanna laugh. "I think he likes her too as he is always smiling when she is around. I reckon they will get married. Who are you going to marry Jo?"

Johanna spluttered as her breath got caught in her throat.

"Shush up Julia, you can't ask questions like that. You are embarrassing Jo. Look how red she is, even her ears have gone pink."

The children laughed as Almanzo pointed at Johanna's face. Trying to hide her embarrassment, Johanna stood. She suggested it was time to move on. They walked for a little while chattering about this and that before the children in front fell silent coming to a sudden halt. Johanna looked up to discover why. What she saw made her heart almost stop beating.

An Indian brave dressed only in buckskin breeches sat on his pony staring at them. As she watched he rode slowly forward, jumping off his pony as he got closer. His shirtless chest was covered in a faint sheen of sweat, his bow and arrows still on his shoulder. Julia and some of the other girls grabbed hold of her skirts, hiding their faces. Almanzo took out his knife and went to stand in front of her. She held him back gently, her eyes locked with those of the Indian. He held out his hand and stared at her.

She took his hand and shook it, not at all sure whether that is what she should be doing. Her instincts were to grab the children and run but there was no way they would all get away. Especially as he had a pony.

His handshake was firm but gentle. She saw his eyes widen as his lips curved into a smile. Glancing down, she saw Julia had stepped forward with a bunch of wildflowers and was holding them out to him. Giving Johanna a quick smile, he let her hand go. He bent down on one knee and took the flowers from Julia giving her hand a quick shake making her giggle.

"You lost?" He asked, his speaking English shocking all of them.

Johanna shook her head as she couldn't find her voice.

"Our wagon train is just over there. With lots of men and guns," Almanzo said in a threatening tone.

At the mention of guns, the smile on the Indian's face faded. He turned to leave.

"Wait please," Johanna said. "Are you thirsty? We have plenty of water and some food." She handed him a small piece of bread.

He looked at her and then at the bread.

"I don't think he ever saw bread before, Jo,"Julia whispered.

Johanna mimicked eating so the brave understood. He took a piece of the bread, smelling it before he put it into his mouth. He chewed for a couple of seconds. "It is good. Thank you."

She gave him the rest of the loaf. "Take it please. We have plenty."

He smiled in gratitude before a pained expression took over as he looked at Almanzo.

"I must go. I do not want trouble."

"There won't be trouble. Our men do not want to fight."

"Yes they …"Almanzo's next word was cut off by Johanna's hand over his mouth.

The Indian looked at her sadly. "Seems some men want blood young."

"Thank you for checking we were not lost. I hope you get back to your people safely."

"I will." the Indian bent down to pick up a buffalo chip. He handed it to Johanna. "Burn this under covers and it will help fight this." He pointed at the mosquito bites on her wrist and neck. "I go now."

He leapt onto his horse and rode away. Johanna watched him go, wondering how an Indian had learned so much English. Once he was gone, she turned to deal with Almanzo. "You were very rude."

"He's only an Indian."

"He is a person and he tried to help us. You should have behaved better. You embarrassed me and yourself. The next time I go walking with the children you shall stay behind. I do not want to associate with people who think the way you do."

A twinge of guilt hit her at the downcast look in his eyes. But he had to learn a lesson. It wasn't right to threaten anyone, particularly someone who had simply wanted to help.

* * *

"WHERE'S YOUR DAUGHTER, I want a word with her."

"Mr. Price, please calm down and stop shouting."

"I want to see your girl, Johanna. Did you know you're raising an Indian lover?"

Johanna stepped forward but her ma pushed in front of her. "Now look here, Mr. Price. Nobody comes to attack my family without just cause."

"Stephen go find Pa. Now," Becky whispered.

"Why don't you take a seat Mr. Price and have some coffee? We can talk about whatever has upset you," Ma continued.

"I don't drink coffee with the likes of you. You girl, you

don't have the right to tell my son off for what he says. I am not rearing a sissy."

"Almanzo is not a sissy Mr. Price. On that much we can agree. But he was wrong today. He embarrassed me and therefore I have told him he is not welcome on our walks." Johanna held her head high. She had done nothing wrong and wasn't going to let this man bully her.

"Did you know they met an Indian on the trail? Your daughter actually fed him and when my son tried to protect her, she chastised him. She told him Indians are real people and as such they don't deserve to be killed.

"That's right. I did tell him that. A lesson you should be teaching him yourself. We are all God's creatures Mr. Price." Johanna wished her voice was steadier.

"Indians ain't got nothing to do with God. The only good Indian is a dead one. You need to keep your dangerous thoughts to yourself. Or if you are so fond of your Indian friends, maybe you should go live with them." Mr. Price's expression changed to a nasty sneer. "Did my son interrupt a lover's liaison."

Johanna's hand stung as she slapped Mr. Price across the face. "You are disgusting. How dare you?"

He grabbed her and twisted her arm painfully behind her back. His face was so close to hers, the smell of bad teeth made her want to gag.

"What's wrong with you? What does a redskin savage give you a white man can't?"

"Respect," Johanna hissed. "The man we met today didn't put a hand on my person. Release me at once."

"And if I don't?"

"I would do as the lady asks, Price. Now." The click of the gun got Price's attention.

He let go of Johanna but pushed her forcibly toward the stranger from the dance. Thankfully his reactions were quick enough to stop her from falling as her foot got tangled in her skirts. He drew her to his side, placing a protective arm around her waist without once letting Price out of his gun sight.

"Are you alright? Did he hurt you?"

"Not really," Johanna hated the fact her voice trembled. The man looked at her quickly before turning his attention back to Price.

"Go back to your wagon Price and stop picking on defenseless women. If Mr. Thompson was here, you wouldn't have dared behave the way you did."

"You are taking the side of an Indian lover over me? You've known me ten years, Rick."

"We go a long way back Tom but I never agreed with the way you treat folk. Miss Johanna is correct. We are all equal in the eyes of our God. I have only met Miss Johanna once but her reputation precedes her. Everyone comments on how kind, courageous and sensitive she is to others. In fact, any man would be thrilled to have a daughter like her. I suggest you take a leaf out of her book and go home and teach that young'un of yours some manners."

"You ain't heard the last of this. I am going to find Captain Jones," Mr. Price spat.

"Do that. You'll save me the trouble. Now get."

Johanna watched with relief as Mr. Price stormed off, muttering loudly. The man let her go - the loss of his strength by her side making her feel worse. Her ma came over and took her in her arms. "Johanna darling, are you alright?"

"I'm fine Ma. The Indian Mr. Price mentioned stopped to check we weren't lost. He didn't do us any harm at all." Tears threatened. Embarrassed enough by the events of the evening, Johanna wanted to run to the security of her tent. But that would be rude.

"Mr. Ellis isn't it? I don't think we have met, I am very sorry about your wife and young'uns. Thank you so much for coming to our rescue. Would you like some coffee?"

Johanna paled at her ma's words. She'd been dancing with a married man? How could he have treated her so well with his wife and children traveling in the same wagon train.

"No thank you ma'am. And the name's Hughes, Rick Hughes. Mr. Ellis is my brother in law. I best be getting back to his young'uns. They get scared if I leave them too long."

"I am sure my husband will be along later to say thank you. He is not going to be happy when he learns how his daughter was treated."

"With respect Ma'am I hope he won't seek vengeance. It is hard enough on this journey without arguments breaking out between us all. Goodnight."

"Mr. Hughes has such a lovely mellow voice. He was

a kind man, the sadness at the loss of his sister and children is evident in his eyes but he doesn't drag everyone else down into his sorrow," Ma said before turning her attention back to Johanna. "You are very pale darling. Mr. Price needs his ears boxed. But in the future, please tell me or your pa if you encounter any more Indians. I am sure Captain Jones would prefer to know if any are nearby."

"Yes Ma,"Johanna answered automatically. He wasn't married, he was the children's uncle. She knew she shouldn't be happy after all he had lost. She couldn't help being relieved he hadn't been married after all.

* * *

LATER THAT EVENING, Captain Jones and David came to visit their wagon. Johanna had been expecting them but she was still nervous.

"Miss Thompson, I came to check if you were alright? I heard there was some trouble earlier in the camp."

"I am fine, thank you."

"I have spoken to Mr. Price and he won't lay a finger on you again. I don't agree with how you were treated..."

"But?" Johanna asked.

"Miss Thompson, I appreciate your views but the fact remains we are traveling across Indian country and not all Indians are friendly."

"This one was."

"Johanna Thompson, don't be impertinent."

Johanna saw the glare her pa sent in her direction but she also caught the quick shake of David's head.

"I apologize Captain Jones. I am still rather shaken up. I should have told you about the Indian. I will do so in future."

"Thank you Miss Thompson," Captain Jones replied. "Mr. Thompson are you happy to leave things alone with Price? I really do not want any more trouble."

"I won't go near him unless he comes near my family again. I have to thank the Hughes man for intervening. Could one of you point him out to me?"

David nodded as Johanna said. "Can I come with you please. I want to say thank you."

"I will come too, Pa," Eva added.

"Becky, Stephen stay with Ma. Girls follow me."

Johanna walked beside her pa allowing Eva walk beside David. She knew her sister wasn't interested in thanking Mr. Hughes as much as taking the opportunity to see David. She couldn't blame her for that. As luck would have it, Mr. Hughes appeared to be on guard duty. He wasn't at the wagon which appeared deserted. Disappointed, she and pa turned back in the direction of their wagon. David and Eva trailing along behind them.

CHAPTER 33

"I can't wait for the fourth of July party, can you, Eva? Ma said there is going to be lots of food."

"Stephen Thompson, is that all you ever think of, your stomach?"

"Yup!"

Eva smiled as the young boy ran off. She envied him his freedom, he seemed to be oblivious to the trials they faced every day. She had to stop thinking like that. At least we will get a few days' rest. It will be a chance to relax a while too. Captain Jones had promised the group if they arrived at Independence Rock prior to July 4th, they could set up camp for three whole days.

The next day, Captain Jones called the group together.

"We did it. We arrived at Independence Rock before the fourth of July. That should mean we get through the mountains before the worst of the weather hits. Everyone has contributed to this achievement. We will camp here for three days. Enjoy yourselves, folks."

Eva watched Captain Jones as he walked away. It was just about the longest speech he had ever given.

"Did you hear that, Eva, we get to have a party. I can go swimming. Can't I, Pa?"

"Yes, Stephen, so long as you are careful. You still have chores to do. Once they are done and your ma doesn't need any more help, off you go."

"You can help me collect some water, Stephen," Eva called to her brother. They walked toward the Sweetwater River.

"It's freezing, Eva."

Eva envied her brother. He could just strip his top off and go swimming. People would have heart failure if she were to follow suit. She contented herself with wading and using some cloth to wash her face, neck and arms. Then she left her brother playing with his friends and headed back to help her ma.

* * *

THE OXEN HAD BEEN LET loose so they could benefit from grazing on the grassy banks of the Sweetwater River while everyone could get caught up with chores. Her pa wanted to carry out a few repairs on the wagon while Ma wanted to get the laundry done and mending completed. There was also the cooking for the big feast planned for the party.

Her ma had invited Milly and Stan together with the

Longs, the Bradleys and the Freemans to eat with them. David had gone hunting to provide the Long's share of the meat. David and a few of the other men came back laden with rabbits, antelope and sage hen.

"Eva, your ma invited us to join your family for the party. I think she knows my cooking skills haven't improved that much."

"Nonsense, Milly, there is no comparison between what you can do now and what you used to know. You hardly ever burn stuff now."

Milly giggled, her hands over her slight bump. "True, but I am not at all sure Stan would trust me to cook an antelope. I wouldn't know how to prepare it to start."

Eva made a face. She didn't mind cooking the meat once it had been skinned and cleaned. Thankfully, her pa did most of it knowing his girls had rather weak stomachs.

"Why don't we have a look through my wagon and you can tell me what to bring to help your ma?"

"Let me just drop this water off first. My arms are getting longer by the minute." Eva dropped the water off to her ma and explained where she was going and why. Then she followed Milly. They collected some Boston baked beans, six eggs and a few potatoes. Milly also had some cans of fruit which she donated.

Eva wondered if Milly knew how long it would take to prepare the feast. They would spend hours roasting and frying the meat as well as preparing fresh bread, rice, potatoes and baked beans. Her ma planned on making some treats too.

"Ma made some fruitcake back in Virgil. She's been saving it for today. That's Pa's favorite."

"What will she make for dinner? Stan is hoping she is making a pie. He said her pastry crust is so light, it could fly to heaven."

Eva was glad Stan was making Milly smile again. For a while, she'd been worried about her friend. Her low mood and pregnancy related illness had left her so weak. Becky had shared her concerns over whether Milly would live through the trip. But she seemed to be blooming now.

"Are you going to climb Independence Rock and carve your name?"

"Yes, Milly, I can't wait. I want to see the names of the other travelers who went before us. Are you coming too?"

"No way. I am not great at climbing and with this precious one, I think I will stay and help out here. I am getting better at peeling potatoes. I manage to only take the skin off now. Well, most of the time."

Eva smiled at her friend's chatter but her mind was caught up thinking of David. He'd asked her to wait for him to return to climb the rock. Joey had asked Gracie to go with him so the four of them would climb together.

When Eva and Milly got back to the wagon they found Johanna and Becky laying a sheet on the ground. Someone had donated a red skirt to make stripes.

"All we need now is a blue jacket."

"I have one. I will go get it now," Milly said excitedly as she turned back toward her wagon. Becky jumped up. "I'll join you."

Eva exchanged a look with Johanna. Typical of Becky to try and get out of the work.

Pa and some of the other men were taking apart their wagon beds to turn them into tables. Ma had insisted they were going to be civilized as possible for the party. Pa was muttering about female sensibilities and the extra work they brought along. Eva knew her pa wasn't really serious. He would do just about anything to keep his wife happy.

* * *

LATE AFTERNOON, all the chores that had to be done were completed to her mother's satisfaction, and Eva was finally able to escape to find David. She'd been fearful Harold may turn up and ask her to climb the rock with him but he seemed to have disappeared. His new friends were also gone. *Maybe they decided to go ahead without us.* Eva hoped that was the case but deep in her heart she knew Harold wasn't that brave. There was safety in numbers, and although the Indians they had seen on route didn't come near them, they were still a potential threat.

CHAPTER 34

David was waiting with Joey Freeman as Gracie and Eva made their way towards them. Joey grabbed Gracie's hand and pulled her along a little ahead of them. David and Eva held hands as they chattered about their day. The climb wasn't difficult but Eva wished she was wearing trousers as her skirt got in the way. David helped her as much as he could. They stopped to read various messages as they climbed. "I wonder if all these people are now living in Oregon?"

David didn't answer her question. He studied the rock but his silence said everything. She knew it was silly to tempt fate but she hoped their good luck would continue. They had been relatively lucky so far.

"Will I scrape your name as Clarke?" David whispered to Eva, standing behind her, his arms wrapped around her middle, both gazing back at the journey they travelled.

"I wish you could," she said softly. She wanted to kiss

him, to feel his arms around her but there were too many people around. "Look at how far we travelled. It looks so pretty from up here, doesn't it?"

"Let's not look back, Eva. Look over there. Somewhere over there is our new home."

"Our home?" She nestled back into his arms.

"Yes, darling, our home. We are going to get married, claim some land and build our home. You are going to grow all sorts of fruit and vegetables in a little plot I will dig for you near the house. We will have some apple trees in our orchard. I will plant crops to start with and then as the years go by, we will expand our house to accommodate our growing family."

Eva blushed scarlet. She watched as David scratched his name and then hers. Her spirits fell when he carved Eva Thompson but rose just as fast as he winked at her before adding on Clarke.

"Someday soon. I promise," he said to her solemnly before kissing her quickly on the lips.

* * *

DAVID HELD HER CLOSE, enjoying the feel of her hair against his chin. She smelled of the soap her ma made, clean and fresh. Her skin was so soft inducing a flood of longing. He closed his eyes, allowing himself to indulge in a fantasy where he was free to kiss her, sweep her into his arms and take her back to his wagon. One day, this beautiful lady would be his wife.

She said he helped keep her fears away. What she didn't know was she did the exact same thing for him. When he was with her like this, his arms wrapped tight holding her close, he could let the worries melt away. He felt more positive, more optimistic for their future. When she was away from him, his mind dwelt on the dangers of the journey ahead of them. They had traveled so far, yet the most trying and dangerous part of their journey lay ahead of them. How many of their party would survive the trip?

Reluctantly, he realized it was time to get back. He didn't want Mr. and Mrs. Thompson to worry. He turned her to face him, allowing his lips to brush hers gently. It took all his restraint not to kiss her properly. "Come on, darling, we best get you back to your parents before your pa gets his shotgun out."

Eva's tinkling laugh sent shivers over his skin. Holding her hand, he helped her climb back down the rock meeting Gracie and Joey on the way. He knew the other couple planned to marry as soon as they reached Oregon. Joey was lucky, Gracie's father had warmly welcomed their relationship, despite the fact Joey had given Mr. Bradley a piece of his mind over the Indian incident. Maybe one day Eva's pa would look at him in the same way, Mr. Bradley regarded Joey.

* * *

RACHEL WESSON

"Ma, you excelled yourself. I think your cakes can be smelled for miles around." Eva could see her ma was pleased with the praise, although she didn't comment. She was busy writing in her diary. Every chance she got, she took out the diary and kept it updated. None of them were allowed to read it—not even Pa.

Eva took the time to write to Granny. She told her all about their preparations for the party including how Becky and Johanna had organized a group of women to make a flag to hang from the rock. Together they had sewn various costumes for the children to wear. All the boys wanted to be Indians, something the adults found amusing. Eva told her granny about the dance to be held the next evening after everyone had eaten their fill.

She hoped to be able to dance with David. It all depended on how her pa was feeling. He seemed to have lost his initial hostility to David, not accepting him exactly but he didn't run him off the way he would have done in the past. Eva was hoping this was a sign of better things to come. But first she had to keep Harold at a distance. He was becoming more trying than usual insisting they set a wedding date.

She thought about their encounter last night and shivered. He had asked Pa if they could go for a walk. She tried to say she was busy but her pa had insisted saying it was no way to treat a hero who had saved Stan's life.

They had only walked for a few minutes before he tried to pull her behind some bushes.

"Harold, please don't."

"Why? It's natural to want to kiss the woman who will become your wife."

Eva decided it was time to stop this misunderstanding.

"Harold, you are a nice man." She almost choked on the lie, but she had to let him down gently. "I don't love you and I will never marry you."

"You will. Your pa is all set for a match between us."

He was so confidant in his reply, she wanted to scream. Instead, she asked.

"Why me? You could have the pick of any woman you wanted. Someone prettier, richer, more accomplished. A woman to fit your role as a rich merchant in a big town."

Harold seemed to consider what she was saying.

"All true but I want you. I always get what I want. You will make me a good wife and mother to our children."

The look in his eyes made her feel ill. She decided it was time to be direct even if it was cruel.

"I am not a piece of candy or a new horse. I am a woman with a mind of my own and I swear I will never marry you."

"Oh, but you will." His tone was steely and the look in his eyes frightened her.

He moved to kiss her but she pushed him so hard he'd fallen over. She hoped he was still hurting. Why did she have to think of him? He had ruined her good mood. She tried to picture David carving her name but her mind was stuck on Harold.

CHAPTER 35

Johanna went for a walk. At least that is what she told herself she was doing but in reality she was looking for Mr. Hughes. She had only spotted him once or twice in the distance since the run in with Mr. Price. She hoped she would have the courage to speak to him should she find him.

She spotted Carrie and Sarah first walking back toward a wagon. She followed them finding Mr. Hughes mending something while sitting on the grass, his back against the wagon wheel. He had a plate of half eaten food by his side but it was so burnt, she couldn't make out what it was. He didn't notice her until she was right beside him. She coughed.

"Excuse me, Miss Thompson. I didn't see you there." He scrambled to stand up.

"Please don't stop working. Can I sit down?" She asked, pleased her voice sounded normal despite the butterflies in her stomach. "I wanted to say thank you for the other day. Pa and I came to see you that evening but I think you may have been on guard duty."

He stayed silent so she continued.

"I apologize for Ma calling you Mr. Ellis. We just assumed..." Johanna let the silence speak for itself. "The children called you Rick. I thought it was odd them calling you by your Christian name but I didn't really think too deeply about it." Johanna knew she was talking too much. It was what she did when she was nervous. She wasn't scared of this man because she thought he would hurt her. It was the way he made her feel. One look from him and her skin started shivering. She wondered what it would be like if he were to...

"I think most people would assume we were husband and wife. Sadie was my older sister. Her husband, Toby headed for Oregon just over a year ago. He wrote to say he had claimed some land and was in the process of building a home. She wanted to be with him. I told her she was too weak with the baby but she wouldn't listen. I should have made her listen. If I had been stronger, she would still be alive. The boys too."

Johanna wanted to hug him to relieve the pain in his voice and remove the shadows from his eyes. But that was not appropriate.

"Can I help you with your nieces? I don't want to push in or be rude but I can see you are struggling."

"Is that a nice way of telling me I am hopeless in the

kitchen?" He looked at the half burnt offerings on his plate.

"No I can see you are a master cook. In fact I should invite my family to sit at your fire," she grinned as he laughed.

"If your family could spare you, I would really appreciate the help."

"They can. I have a twin sister, an older sister and a younger brother. They can help Ma. I can help you and the girls might come out of themselves if they were to come on walks with me and the other children."

"Will you eat with us too?" he asked.

"I can't do that. It's not seemly," Johanna said, her cheeks flushing. "People will talk."

"I apologize. Sadie always said I should care more about what society thinks. Especially in situations like this."

Johanna waited for an explanation.

"I mean, the boredom of the trail is only brightened by gossip. I wouldn't want to cause you to be their favorite topic."

"After Mr. Price's complaint the other day, I doubt you are the reason I will be spoken about. It's more likely the fact I am an Indian lover." Johanna's tone didn't hide her anger.

"And are you?"

She moved back. "What do you mean?"

"Not what you are thinking," he said quickly. "I mean

do you believe what you said. About all people being equal."

Johanna let out a big sigh. "Yes I do. I know it's not a popular opinion but I am not interested in being popular."

"What are you interested in?"

Johanna blushed, she had walked herself into that one. Answering his question would mean telling the truth about her dreams. Yet not answering would be rude.

"I apologize again Miss Thompson. I seem to be continually saying the wrong thing. Sadie was right. I have no place in polite society."

"It's not that. I just never told anyone before. My pa wants me to get married and raise a family. But I..."

"Want to become a missionary?"

"What?"

"Sorry I was teasing. Go on," he said, smiling.

"I want to be a teacher. I love children and they seem to like me."

"I am confused. Why can't you be both? Become a teacher and be a wife and mother."

"No man wants his wife working."

"Now who is being judgmental? Not all men are the same Miss Thompson."

"Rick, Carrie ripped my dress. On purpose."

Johanna was glad of the interruption.

"Are you any better at sewing than you are cooking?" she asked him.

"Much worse I'm afraid."

"Sarah, why don't you change your dress and give me

the ripped one. I will mend it for you and give it back to you tomorrow."

"Thanks Miss Thompson."

Johanna smiled at the young girl. "Assuming it's okay with your uncle, why don't you come back with me to my wagon and I will show you how to sew it. Bring Carrie too."

"Thank you again Miss Thompson. I am on guard duty and didn't want to leave the girls alone."

"I will keep them with us until bedtime. If you aren't finished by then I will stay with them here until you get back."

* * *

"You look different. Did you do something with your hair?" Becky looked at her sister critically.

Johanna shook her head as she picked up a skirt and started scrubbing it hard. She hoped her sister would think the flush on her cheeks was exertion rather than anything else. If Becky got a hint her twin had been thinking of a man, she wouldn't stop for a second until she found who it was. She would love to share her feelings with someone but not Becky. Her twin was so impulsive she may go and tell Rick.

"Your eyes are all sparkling. You look like Eva does when she looks at David," Becky moved her washing tub closer to Johanna. "Who put such a spring in your step?"

"Nobody. You are imagining things. Just because you

are in love with Captain Jones, you expect everyone to be the same."

At the mention of their leader, Becky's face fell.

"Don't mention that man's name again. He is nothing but a...a...I won't say it as it's not ladylike."

Johanna giggled making Becky angry.

"What is so funny?"

"You. Since when have you cared about being lady-like? What did the Captain do now?"

"He had dinner with Gracie and Mr. Bradley."

"It was only dinner. He didn't pick Gracie up and ravish her in the bushes," Johanna scrubbed harder at the look on her sister's face. If she wasn't careful Becky would tip the water tub over her head.

"I don't think that was called for, do you? I was complimenting you on how well you looked today and you reward me by being snippy. It doesn't suit you Jo, not one little bit."

Remorse overwhelmed Johanna. She hadn't meant to hurt her sister.

"Becky, I'm sorry. I didn't mean to be hurtful. Tell me what happened between you and Captain Jones. What's he done to upset you and it wasn't eating with Gracie," she paused at the look on Becky's face. "you never know, I might be able to help."

Becky laughed before splashing some water at Johanna. "How can you help? You know less about love affairs than Stephen does. Since when did any men ever turn your head? You never have it long enough out of a book to notice men."

"That's not true," Johanna protested. She immediately regretted saying anything as a speculative look came into Becky's eyes.

"Who is he?"

"Who is who?" Johanna replied, hoping against hope her sister would stop.

"The man who put the sparkle in your eyes. I knew there was something different about you today. Don't give me some mumble jumble about it being a new book you read. You've met someone haven't you? Was it one of the soldiers? No it couldn't be as it's been days since we last saw them. Is it someone from the train? Come on tell me or I'll tell Pa you've been meeting someone in secret."

"That's a lie. And anyway if you tell Pa anything, I will tell him about you and Captain Jones."

"So there is something to tell."

Johanna prayed someone would interrupt them. She wasn't going to tell Becky anything but Becky wasn't going to give in easily.

She was reminded of her Granny's saying, be careful what you wish for as the last person she wanted to see, appeared right in front of her.

* * *

RICK CAME upon the sisters doing their washing. They didn't notice him so for a moment he stood watching them work. Or rather Johanna work. Her hair had come loose and a few blonde locks were flying loose around her face. He wondered what her hair smelled like? Was it as soft and silky as it looked. He stuck his hands into his pockets in case he lost control of the impulse to reach out and touch her. Just then Johanna looked up and caught his eye. Was it his imagination or did her cheeks turn pinker? He really wanted to apologize for the way he had spoken to her, calling her judgmental but he was loath to do that in front of her sister.

"Mr. Hughes? Are you all right? Is it the girls?" Johanna sounded anxious.

He moved toward her pulling off his hat.

"I just wanted to say thank you for sewing Sarah's dress and for looking after the girls so well. They said your apple pie was the nicest they tasted in a long time."

"My sister is a good cook but I baked the pie." Becky dried her hand in her apron as she spoke. "Nice to meet you Mr. Hughes. Your nieces are lovely girls."

"Thank you Miss Thompson." He turned to go.

"Mr. Hughes, what are the girls doing today? Do they want to walk with us?" Becky asked.

"If that would be suitable they would love to. Young Carrie kept talking about Stephen the whole time. He showed her some bugs and stuff."

Johanna shivered from loathing. She loved animals but drew the line at bugs. Stephen was forever hiding worms or spiders in her bed clothes.

"Are you cold Miss Thompson?" Rick asked seeing her shivering.

"She's just a big scared cat. Stephen keeps putting bugs in her blankets. Jo doesn't much like them."

"I hate them." Johanna said in response to Becky's comment. "I know they are God's creatures too but they wiggle so much," Johanna said screwing up her face.

He could have laughed at the expression of distaste on her face but he didn't. He couldn't hurt her feelings especially after what he had said about her judging everyone.

"I will send the girls up to you. They are very excited about the 4[th of] July party."

"Fine with us. See you then Mr. Hughes." Becky smiled. "Actually why don't you and the girls join us for dinner tomorrow. Our ma won't mind, she is already cooking up a feast."

He wasn't sure what to say. He looked at Johanna but she seemed to find something in her tub very interesting. He was tempted to say no especially given the way Johanna's sister was looking at him with a speculative gleam in her eye. On the other hand, it would allow him to meet Johanna's parents and see more of her.

"If you are sure she won't mind, thank you. My cooking skills are less than adequate. Good day."

"Good bye Mr. Hughes," Becky replied. His gaze shifted to Johanna but she was nearly in the tub at this point. He must have upset her in some way.

Disappointed she didn't even say goodbye, he walked away slowly.

* * *

BECKY WAITED until Mr. Hughes had gone before turning to her sister.

"You've certainly been keeping that quiet."

"Becky, take that look off your face. There is nothing going on."

"Yes there is. He's the man you danced with at Fort Kearney. That was weeks ago. Have you been secretly courting? No, you couldn't have been. I'd have known."

"How could you know?"

"I'm your twin. I would know these things." Becky wasn't sure she would. She didn't know which she was more shocked about. Johanna having a beau or her not knowing about it.

"So how long has it been going on?"

"Rebecca Thompson, there is nothing going on. He just lost his sister and is left with two little girls who have lost their whole family. It's the Christian thing to do."

"There's nothing Christian about the way he looks at you. I know you are naïve but even you should be able to see that."

"I have no idea what you mean. Now can we please finish these clothes?"

"What's taking you two so long. Ma is getting anxious."

"Eva, did you know Johanna has a man?"

"I do not," Johanna protested heatedly causing both her sisters to laugh.

"Sounds to me like you are protesting too much. So who is it?" Eva asked.

"His name is Rick Hughes. He's the man who rescued her from the evil Mr. Price. She's head over heels in love with him. He's quite easy on the eye t..." Becky squealed as water poured over her head. Eva collapsed into a fit of giggles as Johanna stood with her arms on her waist.

"For the last time Rebecca Thompson, I am not in love."

"Who's in love?" David Clarke came upon the sisters, obviously looking for Eva.

"Go away David Clarke. In fact all of you get lost." Johanna's furious tone left David looked at her, his mouth falling open with surprise.

Eva dragged David away as Becky stood staring at the back of her twin who stomped off back in the direction of their wagon. She couldn't remember ever seeing Johanna so angry. She must really have it bad. Becky grabbed a towel to dry herself off all the time wondering what she could do to help her sister's romance move forward. She couldn't leave it to Johanna. She was liable to mess it all up.

CHAPTER 36

espite being on a break, everyone was up early on the 4th of July. The habit of waking to start trekking was ingrained now. Eva and her sisters helped her ma get the table ready. They didn't put any food out since it would spoil in the heat. Instead, they helped drag containers of water up from the river. Their ma organized everything so the dishes that needed to stay cold were closest to the water containers.

Johanna had given up waiting for Becky to help make the flag—instead, relying on a gang of children including the two young girls who had stayed at their wagon the other night. To Eva, it looked like chaos, but Johanna had it all under control. Soon the star-spangled banner was ready.

Captain Jones stood on one of the chairs and read The Declaration of Independence. Then they raised the flag and sang "The Star Spangled Banner." Only afterwards, were they all allowed to sit and eat. Mr. Hughes sat beside David the two of them engrossed in conversation. Becky saw him looking at Johanna but he made no move to approach her. Not that she blamed him as Johanna seemed to be on a mission to avoid him. Thankfully there were too many other people around for anyone else to notice.

The crowd had a great time with everyone complementing Mrs. Thompson on the food.

"Sure wish you could teach my Milly to make a pie crust like this. It is heavenly," Stan said smiling at his wife.

"You give your missus a chance. My Della has been practicing for nigh on twenty years," Pa said, while Eva and her sisters laughed at the mutinous look on their ma's face.

"Any more comments like that, and you will be eating burnt shoe leather for the rest of this trip," Ma pretended to scold her husband, but everyone could see she was joking.

After everyone had eaten their fill, Joey and his pa took out their fiddles and starting playing some music. The women tidied away the food while the rest of the men turned the tables back into wagon beds. The younger children drifted off to play. Once the chores were finished, the dancing could begin.

* * *

Unfortunately, just as everyone was having fun, Harold and his two friends appeared. Harold insisted on dancing with Eva. His friends grabbed Johanna's and Becky's hands and led them into a dance. Eva could have screamed with frustration, and it must have shown in her face as Joey changed the song into an upbeat number which meant plenty of swopping of partners. Eva got to dance briefly with David as he was Gracie's dancing partner. Eva stepped on Harold's foot more than once, but he didn't seem to care. He had been drinking and the smell was making her stomach roil.

It was her pa who had rescued her. A little unsteady on his feet, Harold made the mistake of holding Mrs. Larkin, the wife of Pa's friend, a little too closely. She retaliated by slapping his face. He raised a hand, but Pa stepped in—the anger in his expression making the musicians stop their playing.

"Why has the music stopped, I just started having fun?"

"You manhandled Mrs. Larkin. Show some respect for your elders. I suggest you go for a swim and take your friends with you."

"Mr. Thompson, much as I owe you respect as my elder, you are not in charge of this excursion. Therefore, stop being a stick in the mud."

Harold turned away but before he got a chance to move, Pa put his hand on his shoulder forcing him to turn back to face him. Eva took a deep breath. Her pa was strong but Harold was younger and fitter. Harold saw the raised hand and lifted his fist. David stepped in between the two men.

"Harold, go sober up. You are upsetting the ladies."

"What would you know about ladies, Clarke?" Harold sneered. "I understood you grew up in a saloon."

Eva watched David's eyes widen at the insult and his fists clenched. But he didn't raise a hand. Instead, he said calmly, "Chapman, take your friends and get out of here now. While you are still able to walk."

Harold took a swing but he misjudged the distance and ended up on the ground. The group laughed but stopped immediately as Captain Jones arrived.

"Get out of here now. The children don't need to see grown men behave like this."

"Who's going to make me?"

"I will." Captain Jones put his hand on the gun in his belt. Eva watched Harold's face blanch. Mrs. Larkin was clinging to her husband's arm after one of the children had run to get him. David, Joey and his pa stepped forward with a number of other men in the group. She bit her lip hoping Harold would see sense, although she would be lying if she didn't admit to wishing someone gave him a good slap.

"Go on, Chapman, dip your head in the river and then have some strong coffee. We ride out tomorrow." Captain Jones' stern tone brooked no argument.

Harold must have realized he was outnumbered. He gave the signal to his two friends and they slinked off toward the river.

The music started playing again and this time Eva

found herself in David's arms. She looked around nervously for her pa.

"He took your ma back to the wagon. I guess she was more upset than she let on."

Eva hoped her ma would be alright, but she didn't want to go check on her now. She lay her head against David's chest as they swayed to the music. They were closer than they should have been, but nobody around them seemed to notice. Or perhaps they were just relieved the threat of trouble had gone.

* * *

LATER THAT NIGHT, Eva left the tent to attend to her personal needs. Coming back, she almost screamed as someone grabbed her arm. Harold put his hand over her mouth to stop her from making any noise. He smelled worse than earlier. Her stomach heaved.

"Your pa isn't going to get away with what he did today. I'll make him pay."

Eva twisted her head but his hand was secure. Despite his smell, she bit him.

"You..." He swore, his other hand holding her tight so she couldn't escape.

"Let me go or I will scream the whole place down."

"You are coming with me. I want to engrave our names on the rock."

"I'm not going anywhere. I already put my name on the rock. Let me go or I will scream." Eva didn't want to scream as she feared her pa might shoot Harold this time. He was still very angry over the way Harold had treated his friend's wife.

Harold let her go suddenly so she almost fell over. "I'll show you, Eva Thompson. I am going to go back to Independence Rock and carve both our names on that rock. I will put your real one—Eva Chapman."

Eva ignored him. He could carve himself into the rock for all she cared. She walked back to her parents, for once glad they would be traveling again tomorrow. The good thing about traveling was that Harold usually stayed away from her during the day. At night, she could avoid him by staying in the tent.

* * *

EARLY THE NEXT MORNING, the caravan train set out once more. Everyone was in a good mood. The rest had replenished both man and beast. The men had enjoyed a good feed and were ready for anything. The women had written their letters, got their laundry done and even managed to have some rest. The children were still excited by the party and were now looking forward to more adventures.

As they pulled out, her pa stopped by to say something to her ma. Pa was riding his horse today leaving Ma to drive the wagon.

Eva climbed up onto the wagon to sit beside her ma.

"What did Pa want?"

"He was just asking if I knew why Harold and his two friends Simon and the other man, had stayed behind?"

"Did they?" Eva's heart was beating faster. Surely, he wasn't going back to climb the rock.

"Seems he told Captain Jones he would catch up later today, but he had something to carve on the rock. That whiskey he was drinking has fried his brain."

Eva didn't comment. She wasn't sure whether to laugh or cry. If Harold was successful, he would come back crowing about it. If he wasn't, she would feel guilty she hadn't tried to stop him. Since when could anyone tell Harold Chapman what to do?

CHAPTER 37

By nightfall there was still no sign of Harold or his friends Bill and Simon. Eva didn't like the two men Harold had become friendly with at Fort Kearney. They gave her the creeps if she was honest. Milly had complained to Stan saying they kept looking at her. She was frightened of them. A number of the other women had mentioned how uncomfortable the strangers made them feel. Eva didn't know if Harold knew his new friends were upsetting the travelers, but she didn't think he would care.

With the passing of time, she felt uneasy. They'd been gone too long. It was dark and nobody but the train guards stayed out this late. Given how nervous everyone was about the Indians, Harold, Bill and Simon were likely to get shot by their own people if they tried to come back to the train this late.

"Maybe they found a lot of meat and decided to come back in the morning."

235

"You are probably right, Son. Now speaking of meat, let's eat dinner before your ma burns it to a crisp."

Stephen laughed at his father's joke. His ma never burnt anything.

Eva waited at the back of the wagon looking out over the prairie. She couldn't see anything but despite that she kept looking.

"Are you worried about him?"

David's whisper made her jump about a foot in the air. "You scared me you big eejit," she said crossly. But whether it was cross at being scared or the fact he knew she'd been worried, she couldn't answer.

"He will be back. He has probably wandered off further than he thought."

"I hope so, David. I don't like him but that doesn't mean I want to see him land in the hands of Indians either."

"So you don't like him?"

She pushed him as he teased her. "You know I don't, you—"

She didn't get a chance to finish as he leaned in and stole a quick kiss.

"Go sit by your fire. You shouldn't stand here alone. It's not safe," he said.

She rubbed her fingers across her lips. Looking him straight in the eyes she said cheekily, "So I see." She ran before he could respond, but she heard him laughing softly behind her.

* * *

THE NEXT MORNING, there was still no sign of Harold or his friends. Some in the wagon train wanted to press on to leave as much distance between the train and Indians as possible. Others including Eva's parents, the Longs, the Freemans and Captain Jones wanted to make camp where they were.

"Captain Jones, do you believe the Indians will attack us? Please tell us the truth," Mrs. Freeman asked.

Captain Jones took off his hat to wipe the sweat off his brow. "No, ma'am. I don't. I think they would have attacked already if they were going to. There hasn't been trouble with the Sioux for quite a while now. We haven't given them reason to hurt us."

"Unless those two darn fools did," an older man shouted out.

"I guess we won't know the answer to that until the men come back," Captain Jones replied sternly.

"If you don't think the Indians are going to attack, why are you insisting we all stay together?" the same man asked.

"There is safety in numbers. I am telling you what I think but I could be wrong."

"I vote we stay here. I got laundry and other chores to catch up on as do all the other women. I can fire a gun as can my girls," Ma said.

"I can too, Ma," Stephen piped up.

Captain Jones offered the ones who didn't agree the chance to go on alone but they weren't too keen. After much muttering, they decided to stay with the rest of the train.

* * *

Eva spotted the relief in Captain Jones' eyes. He may not believe the Indians would attack but he still wanted to leave sufficient men to guard the women folk while at the same time providing enough protection for the search party. She hoped David would be one of those left behind.

Before anyone could move, Stephen shouted excitedly. "Indians, look, they're coming, Pa. Will I get a gun?"

"Stephen, whist, will you, I can't hear my own head. Captain Jones, what do you make of it?"

"Everyone on guard. Let's not make any sudden movements, but women and children, try to find shelter in the wagons. Walk slowly."

Captain Jones mounted his horse. Immediately, David followed suit. Eva moved forward, her hand on her mouth, but her ma held her back. "Leave it to the men."

Eva watched as David and the captain rode very slowly out to meet the Indians who had stopped just a bit out on the plain. They seemed to be waiting for something to happen. She watched as Captain Jones tried sign language. Thankfully, there was an Indian who seemed to speak a little more English than Captain Jones spoke their language. The Indians parted ranks that allowed the pioneers to see the missing men for the first time. A woman screamed as the men looked a bit roughed up. But apart from a burst lip and a couple of bruises, they hadn't fared that badly from what Eva could see from this distance.

Captain Jones said something to David who turned back toward the wagons. "They want something," Pa said.

"What is it David? What do they want?" Eva asked.

"They want to see the women and children."

"But why?" Ma said over Eva shoulder.

"They got the impression we were a party of men on our way to join the Blackfeet, another tribe of Indians who are their sworn enemy. Captain Jones reassured them we aren't. They want proof. Indians don't allow their women to go with them on war parties. He's hoping they will leave when they see you women."

Eva stepped forward but her ma pulled her back. "You stay with your sisters and brother. I will go with David. Who is with me?"

A couple of the married women moved forward. Eva saw Sheila Freeman's ma push her inside the wagon. The ladies who volunteered looked grim.

"I ain't letting you out near those savages," Pa said but Eva saw her ma's face tighten.

"Be ashamed of yourself, Paddy Thompson. I didn't marry a man who judges others just because they don't follow the teachings we do. I will speak to you later."

Ma walked out like a soldier prepared to do battle.

"There are some days when I would pay an Indian to take your ma. She has no right to be speaking to me that way."

But Eva knew by the anguished look in her pa's eyes he

was worried sick for his wife. Rightly so, too, judging by the interested looks the Indians were tossing her way.

"They like a woman with spirit," David said softly. Obviously, hoping her pa wouldn't hear him. As luck would have it, the wind carried his words.

"Most real men do lad and that's a fact." Pa started to chuckle. Eva turned to see why only to catch her mother slapping an Indian's hand away as he tried to touch her hair. The Indian seemed mesmerized as her ma showed him the full force of her Irish temper. The other Indians around him laughed and for a second Eva was worried her ma had gone too far. But then the Indian started laughing too.

Captain Jones beckoned David once more and when he came back it was with a demand for some alcohol, skins and ammunition. "Captain says we are to look as if we are searching but we are not to give them more than a couple of robes and some mirrors. Seems their wives love the mirrors the white ladies use. Don't under any circumstances give them alcohol or bullets."

"We don't need any crazy drunk Indians killing us with our own lead," a man nearby said quite loudly causing more than one person to tell him to shush.

"Why did the Indians catch Harold, Bill and Simon?" Ma asked David.

"That's a story I will leave Harold to tell you." David's face was grim.

CHAPTER 38

*L*ater that evening, when Captain Jones finally signaled the train to stop, Eva rushed through her chores.

"Becky, can you do my share tonight? I will do yours tomorrow. I want to see David."

"Go on, give lover boy a kiss from me," Becky said cheekily.

Eva gave her a quick hug before taking off her apron and brushing down her dress. She didn't want to waste time rebraiding her hair. She needed to know what had happened with the Indians.

She found David near the Long wagon. She whistled just like he had taught her. To other people it sounded like a bird but it was their signal to meet. She was a bit surprised to see him walk straight toward her. Usually, he was discreet in case people were watching. Tonight, he didn't seem to care. As he got closer, she saw the anger in his eyes. David didn't often get angry but when he did, he usually took a while to calm down again.

He took her arm, not roughly, but not quite gently either, when he stopped beside her. Was he annoyed with her? She hadn't done anything, had she?

"David, what's wrong?"

He didn't answer but drew her behind some trees.

"When are you going to let me speak to your pa?"

"Not tonight anyway. In fact, I don't think I will stay to speak to you either." She turned to leave but he caught her hand, twisting it behind her back as he pulled her into his arms. His lips claimed hers roughly, his whiskers scratched her skin as his mouth devoured her. She put up one hand to push him away but all resistance melted with the heat between them. She groaned as he left a trail of kisses along the hollow of her neck, up to the smooth curve of her throat before reaching her tender earlobe. She grabbed his shirt closing the slight distance between them. He groaned and jerked her closer as his mouth returned to ravage hers.

Someone coughed in the distance bringing both of them back to reality. He pushed her away, his heavy breathing mirroring hers. She licked her swollen lips as she struggled to speak.

"Can't you see this is torture? Your pa would rather that fool Chapman graced his fire."

She went to rub his arm but he jerked it away turning his back on her. She moved closer, putting her arms around him, laying her head on his shoulder. "I'm sorry, so sorry," she murmured.

"Eva, I want you so much. I need you as my wife. Can't you understand that?" His bleak tone struck her heart. She closed her arms tighter around his waist wishing he would turn to face her but knowing he hated to show weakness.

"When Pa hears the truth about Harold and the Indians, he may change his mind."

"You think? The Indian chief didn't take that long to see his real character. He told Captain Jones he wasn't surprised we wouldn't trade many goods for his safe return. If Harold was one of his braves he wouldn't want him back either."

Eva would have smiled at the chief's words if she had heard them from anyone else. She heard what David left unsaid. If a so called "savage" could read a white man's character so quickly, why couldn't her pa?

She held him tight in silence for a few minutes trying to think of something to say to make him feel better. He turned before she could say anything. Rubbing a finger gently over her lips, he kissed her face all over with butterfly kisses. "I'm sorry I got so carried away."

"Don't be." Eva leaned up to kiss him lightly on his lips. "I love you with all my heart, David Clarke. I will never settle for anyone but you."

David held her close. They stayed cuddling in each other's arms until reluctantly Eva broke away. "I better get back. I love you." She quickly kissed him before picking up her skirts and making her way back to her parents' wagon.

CHAPTER 39

*T*he next week passed quickly. They didn't have any more issues with Indians. They knew they were around because they spotted them in the distance sometimes but they didn't come near the caravan.

"Probably afraid of your ma," her pa had whispered when someone commented on the Indians keeping their distance.

They were making good time and the good weather held. David had come for dinner more than once and the Longs had invited Eva to sit by their fire one evening. Mrs. Long was a wonderful cook, and she had enjoyed listening to Mr. Long's stories as Julia sat on her knee. They passed a trading post belonging to the Salt Lake Trading Company but purchased very little. Pa's preparations had been so thorough they needed very little, unlike some of their company who fell victim to the high prices the store charged for basic provisions.

She was pleased her pa seemed to be tolerating David more. It wasn't much but she was grateful for any improvement. She was also happy her pa hadn't forgiven Harold for his Independence Rock escapade as he called it. Harold had come calling but Pa had sent him on his way much to Eva's relief.

* * *

"Eva, come quick and bring your ma. We need her. There's been an accident."

David's shocked tone and white face told her it was someone he knew well.

Eva's stomach turned over. "Who?"

"Mr. Long. He's been shot."

"Shot?" Who would shoot Mr. Long? He was a lovely man. She didn't have time to ask David anything. He had already raced away.

"Ma, did you hear David?"

Her ma's white face showed she had heard. She reached inside the wagon to take some things out of the medicine box. She also took some white bed linen.

"Becky, watch your brother and sister. Eva, you come with me."

Eva followed her ma but neither of them spoke. They found a group of people around the Long wagon. Mrs. Long was being comforted by another lady, but Eva didn't recognize her. Mr. Long was laid out on the grass, his shirt a mass of blood. Eva's step faltered.

"Come on, girl, he needs our help." Ma's steely tone had the desired effect. Eva stood straighter, ready to do whatever she could to assist her mother.

Eva watched in awe as her ma kneeled beside Mr. Long and started talking to him in a soft voice. His answers took time as he was struggling to breathe. David moved closer to Eva.

"Do you know when your pa and the others will be back?"

"No. Captain Jones said they would be back an hour or so ago."

"Eva, help me, please. We need to get this wound cleaned."

Eva helped her ma as best she could but it was obvious there was little they could do. Ma offered Mr. Long some laudanum but he shook his head. He looked toward his wife. Ma seemed to understand what he wanted. She stood up and drew Mrs. Long over to her husband. Half carrying the distraught lady, she whispered something in her ear, and Eva watched as Mrs. Long took a deep breath and stood straighter. She even tried to smile.

"Leave them be now. They need a bit of privacy," Ma said making everyone draw back.

"Please, Mrs. Thompson, is there nothing you can do?" David's voice shook.

"Sorry, lad, but no. The bullet did too much damage. Maybe if we had a real doctor but I don't think even he could do anything. Were you there when it happened?"

David flushed a little. He wouldn't meet her ma's eyes.

"I asked you a question, David Clarke."

"I wasn't there, Mrs. Thompson. I heard the shot and came running."

"So who shot him?" Ma's stern face would have frightened most.

David looked at the ground. "I don't know. Not for certain."

Eva ached to go to him but she couldn't. Not with Ma looking on. She didn't like the atmosphere. It was almost as if Ma was blaming David. But she couldn't be, could she? David wouldn't hurt anyone.

"Ma, I think Pa and the others are coming." Eva pointed in the direction of some riders.

"You go tell your pa and Captain Jones. I best stay here with Mrs. Long."

A scream from behind them had her ma running to Mrs. Long who was now lying over her husband. Eva had to get away but David's arm stopped her. "You know I didn't shoot him, don't you?"

"Yes, David, but I also think you know who did." She looked him straight in the eyes willing him to deny it but he couldn't. He looked away.

"I hope whomever it is deserves your loyalty," she said before spinning around to go find her pa and Captain Jones. The men were coming nearer.

"What's going on, Eva?" Pa asked.

"There's been an accident. Mr. Long... I think he's dead."

"Dead? How?" Captain Jones asked.

"He was shot."

The men around her pa started muttering. Captain Jones stepped forward.

"Who shot him?"

"I don't know, Captain Jones. Ma came to help him but she couldn't. There was too much blood. It was everywhere."

"Okay, girl, let's be taking you back to our wagon. You need a hot drink. Come on now. Captain Jones will speak to your ma."

Pa led her gently back to their wagon. She didn't know why he was being so nice but she didn't care. She wanted to get the bloodied shirt out of her mind, but it kept wrapping itself around a picture of David's face. He knew more than he was telling.

CHAPTER 40

The entire wagon train spent the rest of the day at the same spot. They didn't have wood to make a proper coffin so his body was rolled in a blanket. The men dug as deep a grave as possible.

Eva watched as a man recited the bible as the body was lowered in. Mrs. Long wrapped her arms around her children who were all crying, the younger ones clinging to her skirts. Eva wiped away a tear as well. She hadn't known Mr. Long well but she'd like him. Not only was he a kind and considerate boss to David, he was also a dutiful husband and loving father. She wondered what the family would do now.

Later that evening she got her answer.

"Mrs. Long has decided she will stay with the train only until we meet some people traveling back. She can't face going on to Oregon without her husband. In the meantime, David Clarke will drive her wagon." Pa said.

David. What would happen to him if the Longs turned back?

"It's very early to make such a big decision. She may feel differently in a few days' time," Ma muttered as she stirred the stew.

"She's not like you. She's not a fighter."

Ma gave Pa one of her looks. "All women are born fighters. Those that have children prove that over and over again."

Pa didn't reply. He seemed stunned by her response to what he'd obviously meant as a compliment.

"There are questions to be answered about the shooting. I am going up to talk to Captain Jones. Girls, help your ma and make sure you go to bed without a murmur. Stephen, are you listening to me?"

"Yes, Pa."

Eva would have laughed at the expression on her brother's face if she wasn't so concerned about the meeting with their leader.

"Pa, can I come with you?"

"No, girl, it's men only. Why did you want to come anyway?"

Eva had to think quickly as Pa's speculative look washed over her. "I just keep seeing Mr. Long lying there on the grass. I can't imagine why anyone would do something like that."

"We will find out. Young Clarke was there. I think he knows more than he's saying. Probably trying to save his own neck."

Eva couldn't stop herself saying no.

"You got something to say, girl?"

"I don't think David would hurt anyone, Pa."

"Hmph." Her father muttered as he strode off toward the men gathering in the center of the circle.

Eva ran to find David knowing her ma would understand. She found him saddling his horse.

"David, you can't leave. You will only make yourself look more guilty."

"They believe I shot Mr. Long." David seemed to be speaking more to himself than to her.

"Tell them who did." Eva could have shaken him at the mutinous look on his face. "This is not a game, David. We aren't in school anymore. You have to tell them."

"They won't believe me." He didn't look up from his horse.

"I will," Eva pleaded with him.

"I can't tell you. It could put you in danger."

Eva struggled to get a grip on her temper. She didn't need protecting now. He did.

"Please don't go."

"Eva, I am not leaving. Whatever else I am, I am not a coward." He didn't let her reply. "I have to go out on rounds." He continued to get his horse ready.

* * *

SHE STALKED OFF. She had to find someone who would listen. She spotted the caravan leader sitting alone at his fire. The meeting must have ended. That had been very quick. She hoped it was a good sign.

"Captain Jones, could I speak to you for a moment, please?"

The captain looked at her for a couple of seconds before nodding. He gestured for her to sit down at his fire.

Eva took a seat, trying to calm the butterflies in her stomach.

"It's about Mr. Long. I wanted to tell you David Clarke didn't shoot him."

"Do you know that for a fact, Miss Thompson?"

Eva wanted to lie but something in the older man's eyes stopped her. She met his gaze. "No, sir. I mean I didn't see the shooting but I know David Clarke and he wouldn't do something like this. He couldn't."

"Is this your heart speaking, Miss Thompson?"

Eva knew her face was scarlet but still she held his gaze. "Yes, sir but also my head. I have known David Clarke since I was five years old and I have never seen him cruel to another living thing be it person or animal."

Captain Jones sat looking into the fire for a while. Just as the silence became unbearable, he spoke.

"I believe you, Miss Thompson. I haven't known Clarke for very long but in that time, I have never seen him display any cruelty to anyone, man or beast. You can tell a lot about a man by the way they treat their animals."

"So you will allow him stay with the wagon train?"

"Yes, miss. I will."

On impulse, Eva moved forward but caught herself just in time. "Thank you, Captain Jones."

"Miss Thompson, your pa know how you feel about Clarke?" Captain Jones looked her in the eye. "I'm not being nosy but your answer could affect my wagon train. I got the impression your pa was hopeful for a match with another man."

"My pa has his own views, Captain Jones. Goodnight." Eva turned to walk away before she embarrassed herself any further. Captain Jones had been very pleasant but people expected girls to obey their fathers. As she walked away, she thought she heard him mutter something that sounded like "Funny how parents can be so blinkered." But when she turned back to look at him, he was once more staring back into the depths of the fire.

As soon as she was far enough away, she picked up her skirts and made her way to the Long wagon hoping to find David getting a couple of snacks for his guard duty. He was there but so were the Long girls.

"Eva, you saved me a trip. Could you return these dishes to your ma, please? She was very kind to cook us another meal."

"Yes, Mrs. Long. She asked me to check if you needed anything else." The small lie tripped off her tongue. She saw David's eyes widen.

"No, she has done plenty. It's about time I got back to looking after my own family. It's what my husband would expect of me."

Eva didn't answer, what could she say? Instead, she motioned to David she needed to speak to him.

"I spoke to Captain Jones."

"Eva Thompson. What did you do that for? You have no right getting into my business."

"Our business, David Clarke, and don't you forget it."

David still looked angry.

"He said he believes you are innocent and would expect you to stay with the wagon," Eva summarized.

"He did?" David's puzzlement made Eva wish she could hug him.

"Not everyone judges you by your pa. Captain Jones only knows you and he likes what he sees. Please tell me you won't run."

"I could never leave you, Eva." He pulled her toward him while stepping into the middle of two of the circled wagons. It offered them some protection. Nobody was likely to see them unless they walked straight past.

He held her close before kissing her gently at first but she let the kiss develop. She wanted him to know she loved him and would never leave him. His kisses left her breathless. Reluctantly, she broke apart from him, both their breathing labored.

"David, I love you. You are never to leave me. Promise."

"I promise, Eva."

CHAPTER 41

The tense atmosphere in the caravan train made everyone nervous. Milly had tried reassuring Eva people didn't believe David had killed Mr. Long. Captain Jones' word was law and he believed David was innocent. A couple of days after the shooting, Captain Jones went scouting ahead. Pa and a group of the men went hunting leaving a skeleton crew of men guarding the wagons. These men included Harold and his friends.

Eva looked up from her laundry. It was impossible to get the clothes clean without decent soap and hot water. All she was doing was wetting them. It would be easier to wear them into the river and take a swim. Given the hot weather, it would be more comfortable, too, but she didn't think her ma would agree with her way of doing laundry. Her sister wasn't having much fun either. Becky was trying to get as much water out of the washed clothes as possible so they would dry quicker. If they weren't dry by the time they pulled out, they would have to wear them wet. There was nothing worse than trying to pull on wet undergarments.

"What's going on over there?" Becky pointed.

Eva followed her finger to spot Harold marching toward David. He tapped him on the shoulder and then punched him in the face as David turned around. David wobbled but didn't fall over.

Eva clasped her hand over her mouth. If David retaliated, he could really hurt Harold being so much bigger than him. Harold deserved it but if David really hurt him, he could get in trouble.

Becky grabbed her arm, dragging her closer to the fight. "Clarke shot Bart Long. I saw him."

Eva stared in horror at Harold but he wasn't looking at her. His attention was focused on David.

The mutterings of the crowd gathered around grew louder. Becky held Eva's arm tighter. "That can't be true? Can it?"

"Of course it's not true. David wouldn't do something like that. He couldn't hurt another person let alone someone who had been so kind to him." Eva's anger made her tone sharper but for once Becky didn't retaliate.

"Of course he didn't hurt anyone. He will be proven innocent. Don't worry, Eva, nobody is going to believe Harold."

But even as Becky said those words, a crowd was gathering threatening to hang David as soon as they found a big enough tree. Eva wished Captain Jones was here but he had gone scouting up ahead. She needed someone fair and impartial.

"Becky, find your pa. Tell him to come back to the wagon quickly."

"Yes, Ma," Becky gave Eva's hand a squeeze before she went looking for their father.

"Eva, I know you are hurting on David's behalf but you need to stay out of this. It's men's business. They don't like when us women interfere."

"But, Ma..."

"For once in your life, girl, stop asking questions and do as you are told." Ma's reprimand was followed by a quick hug. "I know you are suffering but you have to do what's best for David. Now go sit in the wagon with Stephen and Johanna. Teach Stephen his spelling. I don't want him witnessing this mob mentality."

"What are you going to do, Ma?"

"I am going to get Mrs. Long."

"Let me do that, please? You stay with David just in case... What if they decide to..." Eva couldn't bring herself to put David's death into words.

"Find Mrs. Long, hurry back and then go sit in the wagon. I don't think your presence will diffuse the situation."

"Thanks, Ma." Eva hitched up her skirts and walked quickly in the direction of the wagons. She hated dragging Mrs. Long into a discussion about who killed her husband, but David needed all the help he could get.

* * *

By the time she returned with Mrs. Long, the mood of the crowd was even angrier than before. Her ma gave her a pointed look so she headed for their wagon, but as soon as her ma turned her back, she hid behind the nearest shelter. She had to see what was happening. Becky had returned with their pa. Her sister spotted Eva and moved toward her carefully not attracting the attention of their parents.

"What did Pa say? Does he believe Harold or David?"

"I don't know, Sis, I'm sorry. He wouldn't comment until he heard the evidence."

"Harold's lies you mean," Eva spat, fisting her hands. The temptation to wrap them around Harold's scrawny neck was too strong.

The girls watched as their father listened to both Harold and David. He then spent a while discussing things with some of other older men from the caravan.

"We have decided to wait until Captain Jones comes back. Until that time, Clarke will be kept tied up."

The crowd murmured. Some of the men were angry. Bart Long had been a popular man. As far as they were concerned, a murder had been committed, and a witness had identified the murderer. Therefore, all that was needed was justice. Thankfully, a few other people thought David deserved a proper trial and so should be brought to the nearest town. Captain Jones would have the deciding verdict.

Eva watched as David walked toward the wagon where he was to be held prisoner. His shoulders slumped and the look in his eyes showed he had lost faith. She longed to run to him and reassure him everything would be fine. But how could it be? Captain Jones was a fair man but he had said from the start he would act in the wider interest of the wagon train. The mood among the travelers was restless—some were very angry, others were caught up in the excitement of something different happening in their mundane boring lives.

She paced back and forth unable to eat. She had to do something. But what?

"Eva, you are going to make yourself ill. Sit down and eat."

"I can't, Becky. I have to do something."

"Why don't you go see Harold?"

"To slap him?" Eva snapped.

"Well, that's what I would do if I were in your shoes but you are more sensible than that. You know he cares about you. Use that to your advantage."

Eva stared at her sister trying to work out exactly what she was saying.

"Come on, Sis, you can't be that naive. You have something Harold wants. You should be able to make him see sense."

"You mean marry him?" Eva almost choked on the words as her stomach roiled in protest.

"Well...not necessarily."

Eva stopped pacing back and forth to stare at her sister,

her words registering but her brain refused to believe what Becky was suggesting.

"Rebecca Thompson. I couldn't."

"I thought David meant the world to you."

"He does but..."

Becky gave her a look but didn't reply. She returned to where her parents were sitting leaving Eva standing alone. Could she do what Becky was suggesting? If David found out, he wouldn't want her. But if the situation was reversed and she was in trouble, David would do anything to rescue her.

CHAPTER 42

David sat in the wagon, he couldn't do much else, as his legs were bound so tightly. His jaw was throbbing from the punch he'd got. He wished he had a chance to hit Harold back. At least then the other man would be in physical pain. He had gone over and over what Harold could hope to gain by accusing him of murder. Well, apart from his death, how would he benefit from that.

Eva. This had to have something to do with her.

He swore under his breath as he tried but failed to get out of the wagon. He had to find Eva, to warn her Harold was up to something. She may have already guessed but he doubted it. She was so kind. She genuinely believed everyone would see the good in people if they spent time with them. Look how much she believe her pa would come around to the idea of them getting married. David knew he would have to be the last man standing before Mr.

Thompson would agree to let his precious daughter marry a Clarke.

He heard someone whisper his name. His first thought was Eva but he dismissed it. The voice was that of a child.

"David, can you hear me? I brought you some biscuits. Ma made them. She thought you would be hungry."

Tears filled David's eyes. Julia and her ma should hate him the most but they obviously didn't believe Harold. He had never experienced that type of loyalty from anyone before. Well, apart from Eva but that was different. She loved him.

"Thank you, Julia. Could you do something else for me, please?"

"Yes, David."

"Can you tell Miss Thompson, Eva, I want to see her?"

"I will if my ma lets me. She said I have to tell her everything I hear."

David knew Mrs. Long was trying to protect her daughter but did that mean she didn't trust him? But she wouldn't send him something to eat if she thought he had killed her husband.

"Go on back to your ma, Julia. Thanks for the biscuits."

"David, I know you never did anything to my pa. I still love you. You saved my life."

David couldn't reply. She had gone by the time he recovered his voice.

* * *

EVA GOT David's message some time later. She walked quickly toward the wagon where he was being held hoping she wouldn't be intercepted. But she was and by the last person she wanted to see.

"Going somewhere, Miss Thompson?" Harold's face was twisted into a sneer

"Yes, please step out of my way." Eva hid her fears as best she could.

"Now that isn't too friendly, is it?"

Eva gagged at the whiff of his breath. "You've been drinking."

"So what if I have? You should have a drop it might loosen you up a bit. Although from what I hear, you have no issues lifting your skirts for someone else."

The ring of the slap was loud. Eva's hand stung. She turned on her heel intent on walking away, but Harold grabbed her, pulling her behind a wagon out of view.

"You will get away with that one but never raise your hand to me again. You hear?"

Eva stood as straight as she could. Determined to prove he wasn't scaring her, despite the fact her legs were shaking so much, it was a wonder her knees didn't start knocking.

"Take your hands off me you unruly..."

"Now I don't think you want to take that tone with me either. Not when I have your lover locked up." Harold's eyes glittered dangerously.

"He's not my lover."

"No, but you want him to be, don't you? That isn't

going to happen, though, because you are going to marry me."

"I wouldn't marry you if you were the last man on earth." Eva knew it was stupid to rile him, but she couldn't stop herself.

"No? I think you will."

The knowing look in his eyes sent a chill down her back.

"Why do you want me? You could have one of many willing women. There are plenty of girls who want to be Mrs. Harold Chapman."

His chest puffed out at her words but the ugly look in his eyes remained.

"Yes, but I want you. I always get what I want."

Eva tried to edge away from him, hoping to attract the attention of someone.

He grabbed her hair pulling her closer to him. She yelped in pain but he cut off the sound by stealing a kiss.

"That's just a taste of what's ahead of us. You will go back to your pa and tell him you want to get married as soon as Captain Jones comes back."

"He isn't going to let me get married that fast."

"I think he will if you tell him you have anticipated your wedding vows." He pulled her closer again. "Perhaps that isn't a bad idea."

"No, please?" Eva begged. "He won't agree if you do anything to hurt me."

Harold released her reluctantly.

"Find a way to persuade him, Eva. Your lover's life

depends on it."

"Are you saying if I agree to marry you, David will go free?"

Harold laughed making the most evil sound Eva had ever heard.

"When we are married, I will tell everyone it was an accident. Clarke will be spared but I doubt he will thank you. He will see you every day but won't be able to put a hand on you. That pleasure, my dear Eva, will belong to your husband. Me."

Eva moved her head quickly so his lips collided with her cheek.

"You're evil," She spat.

"Maybe, but you're stuck with me." He pulled her closer as he took another swig from his bottle. The smell made her stomach roil again.

"Do we have an understanding?"

Eva hesitated. Could she tell her pa the truth?

"Before you think of telling anyone what happened here tonight, I should say I have two men keeping a very close eye on your sisters. We wouldn't want anything nasty to happen."

Eva couldn't believe this was Harold. How could someone she had dismissed as being a nasty child turn into someone so horrendous? She knew she was beaten.

"How do I know you will keep your promise?"

"You will just have to trust me."

She glared at him but it was the truth. There really wasn't any other option. Not if she wanted to save David.

CHAPTER 43

*D*avid waited but Eva didn't come. Did she believe him guilty too? She couldn't. She knew him. But then why hadn't she come to see him? He tried to release the ropes binding his legs but all it did was chaff his skin. If only he had a knife. He kept twisting this way and that but it only resulted in deeper wounds. He sat back trying to think of a way out of his situation. Somebody had to have seen what happened to Bart Long. Most of the men had been out hunting but the women or children might have seen something. Sometime later he heard a rustling sound. A hand, a female one, had cut a small hole in the canvas.

"Eva?" He whispered.

"It's Becky. Be quiet. We have to move quickly." She climbed into the wagon. He closed his eyes as he realized she had tucked her skirts right up.

He held up his legs while she cut through the ropes. She then released his hands. They hurt like anything as the blood rushed back into his extremities.

"What are you doing here?"

"No need to sound so grateful," Becky replied pouting. "I have to get you out of here. We need to ride for Captain Jones. I have hidden two horses on the other side of the stream. Now I just got to distract the man outside. Meanwhile, you make a run for it. If I can I will catch up. But don't wait for me. Get Captain Jones or some soldiers preferably both."

He watched in awe as she pulled her hair down from it's plait. Then she loosened the top button of her shirt-waist before blowing him a kiss and climbing back out of the hole she had cut. She stuck her head back in. "When you get out, start running. Good luck."

He sat rubbing his ankles and hands trying to get rid of the pins and needles. Why was Becky helping him? They had never been friends at school. In fact, Becky had often got involved with the other children in teasing him. Eva and her sister had got into more than one fight over him. He thought Becky hated him since he seemed to be blind to her charms. He wasn't. He knew she was a beautiful looking girl but his heart was fixed on Eva. Nothing would change that.

* * *

HE HEARD voices outside the wagon. His heart almost stopped. If they came into the wagon to check him, what could he do? He picked up the knife Becky had used. But there was no way he could use that on a man. Then he heard her voice.

"Evening, lovely night for a walk, isn't it?"

"Yes, ma'am," the guard stuttered.

David grinned. He couldn't see Becky through the canvas but he could just imagine her winding the guard around her little finger.

"It's such a pity we are out here in the wilds. I really would like to go for a walk but I..."

"But what, ma'am?"

"Well, it's going to sound funny to a big man like yourself but I am scared. I hate anything wriggly."

"You mean snakes, ma'am? Nothing wrong in that."

"Oh, I wasn't thinking about them. I was just thinking about spiders and stuff like that. I wonder... No I shouldn't impose."

"Please, ma'am, is there something I can do for you?"

David could just imagine the guard begging Becky to let him help her.

"I hope you don't think I am being too forward, but I wondered if you cared to accompany me. A big strong man like yourself would make me feel real safe."

"I don't know, ma'am. I am supposed to be guarding the prisoner." The reluctance in the guard's voice was obvious.

"Oh him. Isn't he all tied up?"

"Yes, but..."

"Well, then a few minutes can't hurt, can it?"

David held his breath as the silence lingered.

"My pa is out on guard duty. Tomorrow night he will be here all evening. I won't get a chance to see the moon."

David heard a sniffle. He wanted to laugh but knew he couldn't. Becky sure had a way of getting people to do what she wanted.

"Oh, miss, sorry, ma'am, please don't cry. I hate it when you ladies do that. I will come with you. We can't be long though. If Chapman finds me gone, he might kill me too."

Too? That guard knew something but now wasn't the time for David to question him. He had to take advantage of the opportunity Becky had set up for him. She was some girl. He hoped she knew how to deflect the attentions of her suitor once they got to see the moon.

* * *

DAVID PEEPED OUTSIDE THE WAGON. The coast was clear. He climbed down, trying to ignore the pain as his legs hit the ground. Chapman's men had given him a few kicks as they tied him up. He hobbled toward the stream. The horses were right where Becky had said. He waited a couple of seconds but when there was no sign of her. He mounted and turned in the direction Captain Jones had ridden out that morning. Was it only ten or so hours since he had last seen the captain. It seemed like much longer. He kept the horse to a gentle walk until satisfied he was far enough from the camp to gallop. He couldn't help wondering why it was Becky who had rescued him. Where was Eva?

CHAPTER 44

*E*va stood shaking in front of her ma and pa. She couldn't bring herself to say the words, yet she knew she had to.

"Pa, I want to get married."

"Go to bed, Eva, now is not the time to be talking about weddings. Not when a young man's life is at stake." Pa didn't look up from the fire.

"No, it has to be now. I have to get married tomorrow."

"Tomorrow. Why?" Eva's ma asked her, watching her face closely. This was it. Could she lie to her parents? Would they not see through her? She couldn't risk them saying no. God only knew what Harold would do not only to David but to Becky and Johanna too.

"Harold wants us to get married quickly. He has..."

"Harold Chapman?" Eva's ma queried, studying her reaction. "Since when have you been agreeable to marrying Harold?"

"He's been a gentleman on the trip, and he can set me up in a proper home." Eva stared over her ma's head looking for inspiration. She saw the washtub. "I am fed up washing and toiling every day. I want a nice home with indoor plumbing. I don't want to ever fret about money again. I want to live in comfort."

Her pa didn't say anything but stared at her in silence. Her ma wasn't biting though. "Eva Thompson, if your sister Becky stood in front of me and announced she wanted to get married tomorrow, I wouldn't be that surprised. She has always had an impulsive streak. But this isn't in your character. You never do anything without considering it from all angles. I don't believe for a second you are marrying Harold Chapman. Well, not out of choice anyway."

Pa glanced at her ma before turning his attention back on her. His eyes seemed to pierce the very center of her soul. She couldn't hide the lie from him, so she didn't meet his gaze. Instead, she stared at his boots.

"Eva Louise, you need to sit down and tell your ma and me what's come over you. There is no way this was your idea. I will admit I had thought Harold Chapman had the potential to be a match for you. But...well, let's just say I have seen a few things that made me reconsider that idea. The answer is no. We won't agree to this wedding."

"But, Pa, you have to. You must."

"I don't have to do anything, girl, you watch your tone. I won't have my daughters speak—"

"Shush would ye, Paddy? Can you not see the girl is

distressed? Eva, what is it? Please tell us, darling. We might be able to help."

Her ma's soft tone had more impact that her da's anger. She struggled but the words wouldn't come. How could she tell them what Harold had threatened? They wouldn't believe her, it was simply too awful.

"Ma, I have to get married. Please, you must agree."

"What do you mean have to? Are you trying to tell me you and Harold have already..."

Eva didn't want her mother to put it into words. She nodded making both her parents gasp. Her pa slapped her across the cheek.

"You harlot. How dare you? What example is that for your sisters and brother? Where is that fella?"

"Don't. Please, Paddy" Eva saw her ma hold her father's arm. "There is a chance you could be having a baby?"

Again, Eva nodded this time her eyes full of real tears. Her parents would think she was ashamed.

"Nothing for it then, girl. You've made your bed, now you can lie on it. I suggest they get married as soon as possible. We don't want anyone talking about a rushed wedding. We set off on this trek to start a new life and you, young lady, were against it from the start. But I never thought you would go this far to sabotage us all."

Hearing her mother voice such a low opinion of her was the last straw. She mumbled an apology and ran to the trees where she emptied her stomach. She fell to her knees as if begging for help. Johanna arrived a little while later with a cup of water and a small cloth.

"I don't believe any of that story you told Ma and Pa. What's really happened?"

Sweet Johanna. She would suffer terribly at the hands of Harold's friends if Eva didn't do what Harold wanted.

"Thanks, Jo." Eva sipped the water. Her stomach was still churning and she didn't fancy being sick again. Her sister had wet the cloth and was rubbing her forehead gently.

"Eva, tell Ma and Pa the truth. They will understand. You can't marry Harold when you love David."

"I have to."

"Your baby, if you are having one, deserves to know his real father. Marry David. Once he's proven innocent obviously."

"What?"

"I heard you talking to Ma and Pa. I know you have... you know what I mean. I don't blame you. Or David. If Pa hadn't been against you from the start, you would have been married by now. But I don't understand why you could even look at Harold."

Eva opened her mouth but Johanna got there first.

"I know what you told Ma but that's a load of old rubbish. You don't care about fine houses or anything like that. You would live in a shed if you could be with David. Please, Eva, tell me. I can keep a secret."

"I can't, Jo. I'm sorry." Eva whispered. "Please leave me now."

Johanna stood up. She handed the cloth to Eva. "We are your family and we love you. Trust us to help. Please."

Eva watched her walk away, dying to run after her and tell her everything but she couldn't. As if he heard her thoughts, Harold appeared.

"You are quite the actress, my dear."

Harold's remark proved he had been watching her closely. She had to swallow hard to stop being sick all over again.

"Now, I best find someone in the caravan authorized to do weddings. Let me escort you back to your wagon first. I must make my apologies to your parents."

Eva tried not to flinch as he caught hold of her hand. Wrapping it under his elbow he walked her back to where her parents stood waiting.

"Mr. Thompson, Mrs. Thompson, I do wish the circumstances were different. I completely understand you are very angry with both of us. All I can say is that your daughter's beauty and kind nature proved too much temptation for me. The fact she wasn't exactly unwilling didn't help."

Eva gasped. She saw her pa's fist clench and her mother putting her hand on his arm. She looked up, catching her ma's gaze. That was a mistake. Instead, of the anger she expected, she saw dawning comprehension. Her ma knew something was wrong. Eva tried blinking rapidly to send her a message to stay quiet. Her ma looked away so she had no idea whether she had made herself clear or not.

"You will get married tomorrow. As soon as Captain

Jones is back. I am sure he has the authority to perform a wedding," Pa said, turning his back on both of them.

Harold smirked at her as he bent to kiss her. She steeled herself against his advance. She wanted to run away screaming don't touch me but instead she stood rooted to the spot. She didn't move a muscle not even when he whispered how much he was looking forward to the wedding night.

And then he was gone. She couldn't stay with her parents another second but fled to the tent. Thankfully, it was empty. Burying herself under the covers, she pretended to be sleeping. Instead, she was crying her heart out only silently, so nobody would hear.

CHAPTER 45

She must have fallen into an exhausting sleep because the next thing she knew she was being woken by her ma.

"Becky's missing. Johanna didn't come back either although I think she said she was minding Mrs. Larkin's children. What is going on Eva?"

Eva stared at her mother. Could she tell her or would Harold carry out his promise to hurt her sisters? But maybe he already had them. She opened her mouth and then closed it again.

"Eva, what is it?"

"I can't tell you, Ma. If I do, something bad is going to happen."

"Did he threaten your sisters? Is that how he got you to agree to the marriage?" Ma asked quietly, her hand rubbing the back of Eva's neck. Nobody outside the tent could have heard her. Eva nodded, not wanting to say anything for fear he was listening.

"Do you know if he has Becky?"

Eva shook her head.

"Johanna?"

Again, Eva shook her head, the tears rolling down her cheeks. Her ma wiped them away tenderly and pulled her close. "You just play along like you been doing. You leave everything else to your ma. Understand?"

Eva nodded before hugging her ma so close she thought she might break her.

"Okay, sweetheart, you got a wedding to plan. So let's get up and get ready. We can't have the bride show up late." Ma spoke loudly enough to be heard but not so loudly that anyone would suspect something was wrong.

Eva rose, her ma squeezing her hand tightly. Even with her ma pretending to go along with it, she wanted to run away. She couldn't stand the thought of getting ready for a wedding where the groom wasn't David.

She followed her ma down to the river where they found Johanna with the younger of the Larkin children.

"Sorry Ma but Mrs. Larkin is still feeling so ill. You would think she would be better. It's not like she hasn't had a baby before," Johanna chattered on but she kept looking at Eva. "You aren't letting her go through with this Ma, are you?" Johanna didn't hide her frustration.

"Stay out of things that don't concern you, Johanna Thompson. Your sister has made her choice. Now, take those children back. We need your help today. It's not every day we have a wedding to prepare for."

"But, Ma, Mrs. Larkin is—"

"Mrs. Larkin has a family of her own to look after her. Do what I say, Daughter."

The look on Johanna's face would have made a good picture if Eva was in the mood to laugh. But this was serious. Where was Becky? Did Harold have her?

When they got back to the camp, chaos had broken out.

"The murderer escaped. Looks like he had help too."

Mr. Bradley's accusing gaze fell not on Eva but on her ma.

"I hope you are not accusing me of any wrongdoing, Mr. Bradley," Mrs. Thompson said, her tone telling Mr. Bradley there would be dire consequences if he was.

"Not you, Mrs. Thompson, but your wayward daughter. She hasn't shown her face yet I see."

Eva sneaked a glance at her ma. Her face was like thunder, her hands on her hips.

"Out with it, Bradley. What are you accusing my girls of?"

"Where's your Becky? She hasn't been seen since late last night. Someone cut into the wagon where Clarke was being kept. They released him."

"Becky is still asleep. As for Clarke, I thought that wagon was guarded."

"It was but nothing has been seen of the guard either."

"And I supposed you think my Becky released Clarke

with one hand and did away with the guard with the other?" Ma's fierce expression made Bradley take a step back.

"What's going on now?" Pa roared.

"Go on, Mr. Bradley. Tell Becky's pa what you think she has done."

Mr. Bradley turned white right before Eva's eyes. His hat twirled in his hands as he walked backwards. "My mistake. I shouldn't have said a word. I apologize."

He was gone before Pa reached them. "Anyone care to tell me what is going on?" Pa glared at Eva.

"Becky hasn't come home. Seems Mr. Bradley thinks she helped David Clarke escape."

"Wait till I get my hands on that girl. As for you, you are the one who brought all this trouble on our house. Are you happy now, girl?" Pa was still roaring.

Eva covered her ears.

"You leave her be. She isn't the one responsible for this mess. If you hadn't kept encouraging Chapman none of this would have happened. Because of you, we will have a drunk in the family."

Eva watched her ma tear into her pa. She didn't know who was more surprised. Ma grabbed Eva's hand and dragged her to the wagon.

"Come on, girl, we have to get you dressed." Ma turned quickly. "Get away from here, Harold Chapman. Don't you know it's bad luck for you to see the bride before the wedding?"

"Sorry, Mrs. Thompson, I couldn't resist."

"Try harder." Ma all but spat at her soon-to-be son-in-law, leaving Pa standing at a distance rubbing his head.

Harold gulped giving Eva a hard stare. She looked straight back at him. Then he smiled but his eyes remained cold. "Captain Jones returned about five minutes ago. He said he would be ready to conduct the ceremony in an hour."

* * *

EVA'S STOMACH ROILED. This was it. There was no escape. She let her ma wash and dry her hair before she pulled a beautiful white dress from one of the boxes in the wagon. "I've been saving this for your wedding day since you were first born."

Eva fingered the dress. It was so beautiful. The shirt-waist was made almost entirely of lace sewn over the satin bodice. It had a high collar. Her ma had attached a small broach. "Your grandmother gave me that for your wedding day."

"It matches the dress."

"It should do since she helped me sew it. This dress was a labor of love supposed to bring you best wishes on your wedding day. Neither of us ever thought you would end up being married by..." Her ma broke down crying. Eva couldn't stop the tears either.

"Ma, please don't cry. I will be fine. I am strong like you."

They cried for a couple of minutes before Ma took a

deep breath. Taking Eva by the shoulders, she stared into her eyes.

"Eva, I can't let this happen. I won't."

"You might not have any choice. But thank you for trying." Eva kissed her ma on the cheek before saying in a forced voice. "Can you help me put it on? I am afraid I will tear it."

Ma helped her get dressed, and then she arranged her hair loosely around her face. "You look beautiful, darling."

Eva kissed her ma's cheek. "Thank you. For everything."

* * *

EVA STOOD WAITING in the tent. Her pa would come to collect her to give her away to Harold. In a couple of minutes, she would make her vows to love and obey a man she despised. Her instinct was to run but she had to suppress it. She wanted to run and keep on running, putting as much distance between herself and Harold as she could. But she didn't take a step. She knew he wouldn't let her go. He would find her and make her life unbearable after he hurt her sisters. If there was one thing Harold was, he was a man of his word.

CHAPTER 46

*P*a came to get Eva, not looking at her as he held the tent door open. She moved to his side. She couldn't have spoken even if she wanted to. He gave her his arm and she took it gratefully. She was furious with her father but she didn't think she would be able to walk alone. She moved slowly toward where Captain Jones was standing. She couldn't look at Harold.

"Before I begin, are you both sure this is what you want? We are bound to meet a preacher in one of the trains on the trail."

"We need you to marry us. Fast!" Harold said pretending to whisper but in a voice that carried. There were murmurs in the crowd. Eva was too embarrassed to say anything. She looked at a spot on a tree in the distance behind Captain Jones' head.

"Miss Thompson?"

Eva didn't respond. She hadn't heard him.

"Miss Thompson, Eva?"

Harold poked her so hard she yelped. She quickly turned the sound into an apology. "Sorry, Captain Jones, I'm nervous. I do."

The crowd laughed causing Eva to look up. Harold was glaring at her but Captain Jones simply looked amused.

"We haven't gotten to that part of the ceremony yet. I was just asking were you sure this is what you wanted."

"I... well... Yes," Eva stammered as Harold continued to glare at her. "Please continue, Captain Jones."

"Dearly beloved we are gathered here today to join this man and this woman in holy matrimony. If anyone here present has a reason why they shouldn't be married, please raise your hand. Yes, Miss Thompson?"

"I didn't say anything." Eva responded.

"I meant your sister Johanna."

Eva whirled around. "Johanna, stay out of this."

Johanna ignored her. "Captain Jones, I don't know why Eva is doing this but she can't marry him. She is in love with someone else."

"Ignore her. She's a child and obviously has been reading too many fairy tales," Harold sneered. "We want to get married, don't we, darling?"

Eva didn't respond. She couldn't. Not even when he glared at her. He took her hand as if he was caressing her but she felt the pressure. He was warning her. She looked around her at her family and then back to his face.

"Johanna is mistaken. Please continue," she whispered.

Captain Jones gave her a funny look. Then he dropped the bible. It took him a few minutes to find the right page again. He started the ceremony again much to Harold's annoyance. "Can't you go any faster?"

"No, Chapman, I can't. This is my first time getting married, and I don't want to mess it up."

The crowd laughed again. Captain Jones corrected himself. "What I mean is that this is my first time marrying someone. Actually, I am not even sure I am allowed to marry anyone. What makes you think this would be legal?"

"Get on with it, Jones." Someone, she guessed it was Harold's friend, said from the crowd.

The sound of a bugle rang out. Then shots were fired.

* * *

"Take your hands off my girl."

"Arrest that man he's a murderer," Harold shouted out, pointing his hand at David. David swung down out of his saddle and punched Harold in the face. Everyone heard the crack of bone before blood pumped out of Chapman's nose. A couple of men ran forward to grab David by the arms but the captain in charge of the guard shouted at them to stand back.

Eva ran into David's arms, sobbing.

The captain also dismounted. "Good morning, Miss Thompson. Seems you still have too many fiancés."

"Captain Wilson," Eva managed to stammer before Captain Jones clapped him on the back.

"About time you lot showed up. Cutting it a bit close, weren't you?" Jones said to Wilson.

"You knew. All this time?" Eva whispered.

Captain Jones nodded. "I am not usually so clumsy, and I think I could marry someone in my sleep given how many times I have conducted the ceremony.

"But why? How?" Eva was so confused.

"Me!"

"Becky? Is that really you?"

Becky grinned broadly out from under her soldier's hat. She was wearing the full uniform including the trousers. "Sorry, Ma, but I had to borrow some clothes. My dress got into some difficulties at the hands of his friend."

"Arrest this man for murder and blackmail," Captain Jones demanded pointing at Harold.

"You can't do that. You have no proof," Harold screeched.

"Actually, we have," Wilson replied. "Your friend gave us a full statement. He was more than happy to tell us everything."

"You can't believe his word over mine. I am a well to do merchant from a good family. Anyone can attest to that," Harold whined.

Eva wanted to slap him. Instead, she hung onto David not willing to let him go. She watched in amazement as her ma stepped forward and slapped Harold on the nose. "That is for my girls. And this is from me." She slapped him again so hard he fell over. Everyone was laughing hard by now.

"Can someone please tell me what is going on?" Pa asked, looking bewildered.

* * *

DAVID STOOD with his arm around Eva.

"Mr. Thompson, Harold Chapman murdered Bart Long. Mr. Long knew he was short changing our fellow travelers and he challenged him over it. He should have waited until there were more of us present but being an honorable man he never expected to be killed. I came back from hunting to hear loud voices. Before I could react, a shot had been fired and Mr. Long was dying."

"You knew all along who it was?" Pa accused.

"Not for certain. I guessed it was Chapman but I had no proof. Nobody was going to take my word over his." Although David didn't say least of all you, everyone knew that was what he meant. Eva saw her pa's face redden.

"You still don't," Harold said smugly.

"Actually, we do now thanks to Becky, I mean Miss Rebecca Thompson. When she came to rescue me, she got the guard talking. He confirmed he didn't want to be killed too. Turns out he witnessed the crime."

"He is just staying that to save his own neck," Harold snapped.

"Maybe he is but given the amount of trouble he is in, it won't work. He was more than helpful. Some of the children witnessed your row with Mr. Long but they have been too scared to come forward. Other people knew you were cheating them but were also living in fear of your threats. Your biggest mistake came when you threatened my girl." David aimed a kick at Chapman.

"She isn't and never was your girl. Tell him, Eva. Tell him how we have already anticipated our wedding vows," Harold sneered.

Eva stepped toward him but her ma grabbed her.

"Mind the dress," her ma whispered.

"Let me. I ain't wearing a wedding dress."

Becky, aided by her twin, attacked Harold. One of the girls threw a bucket of cold water over him and the other one followed with a load of buffalo chips.

"Now you smell just as bad as your insides are. Pure evil," Johanna said looking down at him with an expression of distaste.

Eva looked into David's face. "I swear the only reason I am standing here is because he threatened my family. He said he would...the twins would be hurt by his men. He watched everything. I was scared."

"You have no reason to be scared anymore. Chapman is going with these soldiers and we never have to see him again."

Mrs. Thompson came over to hug David. "I am glad to see you, David, love."

Then she turned to Captain Jones. "Is it true you married lots of folk?"

"Yes, ma'am."

"Then what are we waiting for. We have a beautiful bride in her wedding dress, a handsome, if poorly dressed, groom and a huge gathering of friends and family. I think a wedding is in order."

"But, Della?"

"Shush up, Paddy. I birthed her not you. She has our permission."

"Yes, dear."

Eva grinned up at David at her pa's remark.

"Will you do me the honor of becoming my wife, Miss Thompson?"

"Yes, please," Eva said, beaming.

* * *

CAPTAIN JONES WAITED until Harold had been secured by the soldiers then he invited them to join the congregation to celebrate the marriage of David and Eva. Pa walked her down the makeshift aisle. Once they reached Captain Jones, he kissed her on the cheek and whispered. "I am sorry I doubted you, my Eva," then handing her to David he said, "you best look after her, lad."

Eva thought she saw his eyes glistening but she must be mistaken. Her pa never cried.

The ceremony passed in a blur. And then Captain Jones announced they were man and wife.

* * *

A MAN TOOK out his fiddle and started to play, another man brought out his harp and a third his spoons. As soon as the music started, people started clapping. Some of the braver ones began dancing.

"It looks like a version of the Irish reel. Come on Della, let's show them how it's done."

Pa dragged their ma to the dancing area despite her protests. Soon after David and Eva joined them. Becky asked Captain Jones to dance leaving Johanna standing alone her foot taping along to the music.

"Miss Thompson, would you like to dance?"

She smiled up at Rick Hughes as he pretended to bow. They were both laughing as they tried to keep up with the other dancers. The dancing became so fast, the older ones had to sit out on unturned carts and blankets. The younger people danced and danced.

"I am having so much fun. I feel rather guilty." Rick whispered as they danced.

"Don't feel like that. I am sure your sister would prefer you to live your life. The ones who survive this trip have to live the dreams of those who don't."

"You are very sensible Miss Thompson."

"Not really, I am just repeating something my granny told me before we left Virgil."

There wasn't much time for talking due to the speed of the dancing and the fact that they kept swapping partners for the various jigs and reels. Rick left before the festivities were over as he said he had to check on the girls. Johanna watched him go, wanting to run after him but forcing herself to stay where she was. As her ma had often told Eva, men preferred to do the chasing. She sat out the rest of the dances preferring to watch Eva and David, who looked so happy it made her want to cry. Someday that might be her and...

"They look lovely don't they? So happy." Becky squeezed Johanna close.

"You look better now you are in your own clothes. You had quite an adventure."

"Johanna, you have no idea how good it feels to act and dress like a man. Just for once to forget about skirts and manners and everything." Becky's dramatic sigh made Johanna smile as she hugged her twin close. Maybe she would find her prince charming too. As she followed Becky's gaze to Captain Jones, she couldn't help thinking Becky's biggest adventure was yet to come.

* * *

LATER AS THE newlyweds walked to the wagon which had hastily been cleaned out for them and converted to a bridal suite for the night, Eva stopped her new husband.

"I just wanted you to know what Harold said, you know about anticipating our wedding vows, that was a lie too."

"Thank you for telling me but it wouldn't have mattered. I love you, Eva Clarke. I always have and I always will."

Before she could say anything, he captured her mouth with a kiss so intense it was bruising. She didn't care. She wanted more. She buried her hands in his hair, her mouth openly exploring his. As his breathing quickened, she moved her lips all over his face as if committing his facial features to memory. His heart beat faster as his arms tightened around her. She knew they would never be apart again. She kissed his jaw, his neck, his cheekbones and then finally reached his lips. He kissed her tenderly, a softness developing between them. They had all the time in the world to explore the depths of this love between them. Their kisses deepened, an intensity growing between them like a match dropped on kindling. David groaned before swopping her into his arms and carrying her into the wagon.

"I love you, Mrs. Clarke."

"Show me," she sighed, looking up into his eyes darkened from desire.

"Yes, Ma'am."

* * *

THANK you so much for reading the first book of the Trails of Heart series. I hope you will enjoy the continuing stories of the Thompson girls and the people who come in and out of their lives. The next story is about Eva's sister, Johanna.

JOHANNA THOMPSON UNDERSTANDS her father's wish to go to Oregon.

Can she use the time together to convince him to let her follow her dream?

Rick Hughes inherits two small children, a wagon and a dream to go to Oregon.

But it's not his dream.

Johanna and Rick need to work together to save their families from disaster but doing so could comprise both their dreams. Can they find a way to overcome the difficulties on the trail and find a new life together? Find out more now. Oregon Dreams

AFTERWORD

These stories are inspired by true diaries, not Hollywood movies. The Indian's didn't attack the initial wagon trains. It was only when smallpox and similar diseases decimated the Indian communities and the travelers kept coming, that the raids began. But not in the time period referenced in this book.

ACKNOWLEDGMENTS

This book wouldn't have been possible without the help of so many people. Thanks to Erin Dameron-Hill for my fantastic covers. Erin is a gifted artist who makes my characters come to life.

I have an amazing editors, Julia and MacKenzie, and also use a wonderful proofreader. But sometimes errors slip through. I am very grateful to the ladies from my readers group who volunteered to proofread my book. Special thanks go to Marlene, Cindy, Meisje , Judith, Janet, Tamara, Cindi, Nethanja and Denise who all spotted errors (mine) that had slipped through.

Please join my Facebook group for readers of Historical fiction. Come join us for games, prizes, exclusive content, and first looks at my latest releases. Rachel's readers group

Last, but by no means least, huge thanks and love to my husband and my three children.

ALSO BY RACHEL WESSON

Orphans of Hope House

Home for unloved Orphans (Orphans of Hope House 1)

Baby on the Doorstep (Orphans of Hope House 2)

Hearts at War

When's Mummy Coming

Revenge for my Father

Hearts on the Rails

Orphan Train Escape

Orphan Train Trials

Orphan Train Christmas

Orphan Train Tragedy

Orphan Train Strike

Orphan Train Disaster

Trail of Hearts - Oregon Trail Series

Oregon Bound (book 1)

Oregon Dreams (book 2)

Oregon Destiny (book 3)

Oregon Discovery (book 4)

Oregon Disaster (book 5)

12 Days of Christmas - co -authored series.

The Maid - book 8

Clover Springs Mail Order Brides

Katie (Book 1)

Mary (Book 2)

Sorcha (Book 3)

Emer (Book 4)

Laura (Book 5)

Ellen (Book 6)

Thanksgiving in Clover Springs (book 7)

Christmas in Clover Springs (book8)

Erin (Book 9)

Eleanor (book 10)

Cathy (book 11)

Mrs. Grey

Clover Springs East

New York Bound (book 1)

New York Storm (book 2)

New York Hope (book 3)